Mirror Soul

Book Two of the Unfulfilled Promises Series

By Nancy Cooper

Mirror Soul

Copyright Nancy Cooper 2021

Edited by Katherine Cooper-Restaino and Morgan Miles

Cover photography by Lexi Hanrahan
@lexihanrahanphotography

Cover design by Jacqueline Sweet

For more information about the author and the work she is doing to help women heal their Witch's Wound please visit www.thenancycooper.com

To my beloved Michael.

I have loved you every day of my life and for so much longer.

I will continue to do so until my dying breath.

My hope is that we are to meet again.

If not in this life, then in the next, or on the other side.

Until then.

Contents

PREFACE

White.

Everything was white.

Again.

I looked around as a gentle, cool mist swirled around me.

This felt so familiar to me.

I knew this place. I had been here before and this time, instead of fearing the white mist that swirled around me, I inhaled it deeply and closed my eyes as I felt the mist lick the insides of my lungs only to be pulled into my blood stream like a potent drug. This was the feeling of wholeness. This was the feeling of home. Being in this space was like a warm, beautiful embrace filled with love, acceptance, and peace. It was as if I was actually able to inhabit my true conscious state of oneness and love by being here, in this space.

I knew I was in the astral plane. Where exactly in the astral plane, I had no idea. But I knew at some level it didn't matter because things didn't work that way here, and by being here, in this space, I was everywhere and everything.

But why was I here? I began wracking my brain, trying to figure out what had happened and how I got here. Alas, nothing came to me. It was as if this was the only thing that existed. Right now, in this moment, there was nothing else but me, this place, here and now. I assumed the answers to the questions I needed to be answered were somewhere in this space, so I began looking around.

I wandered slowly through the mist and allowed it to caress my skin as its energy danced with my cells. As I watched the mist swirl around me and gently lick at my fingertips, I began to think more deeply about why I was here. I'd gotten so caught up in actually being back in this space and enjoying the sensations of feeling whole and home that I hadn't really been open to receiving information about how I got here, or why.

It was as if there was some part of me that didn't want to access the information. There was some type of mental blockage there.

Hmm… Why would my mind be doing that, *I wondered?*

If I couldn't get the information directly, I figured I would try a more roundabout approach. I though back to my first experience with this place. I had been scared and uncertain until I met a man who comforted me.

Yes, that's right.

This was where I had first reconnected with Michael before our souls found each other again in the physical plane.

Michael…. *Or now Henry in his current life.*

Oh my god! Where was Henry?! What happened?!

Just as I began to call out for him or to see if anyone else was there, I saw someone walking towards me. For a moment I thought it must be Henry, but that hope quickly vanished like a candle that had just been blown out before it could even fully catch. I did not recognize the energy signature of this person, so I squinted through the mist, trying to get a clearer view of them. Of course, it didn't help.

The shape slowly came into focus as the mist separated ways on either side to let them through. It was in that moment that I realized that the white I was seeing wasn't from the mist itself. It was caused by the mist being illuminated by a light that was shing behind this person. The light shone clearly as a spotlight on them, lighting the way to me. Or perhaps, lighting my way towards them?

When the person stood just a few feet in front of me, I was able to get a good look at them. The person was male and he looked positively ordinary. One of those people who doesn't stand out, nor do they blend in. Someone you can't help but notice, and then you forget them mere moments after you connect. Even now I couldn't describe him. It was as if his looks were subtly changing and morphing as I watched him.

"Why am I here again? What happened?" I asked with confidence that surprised me, not even waiting for him to address me.

He smiled gently and responded by spreading his arms wide as if to embrace me. Then stepping forward, he did just that as he wrapped his arms around me, and whispered in my ear, "Your spirit has been released back into the astral plane again because the body you were inhabiting died."

He said this all so matter of factly, as if it was a totally normal and casual thing to discuss. Meanwhile I simply stood there, still and stiff as a board in this odd man's embrace, for a moment, as his words sunk in.

Vivien's body died?

I tried to remember how or what happened, but I just couldn't. It was as if the information was locked tight in a vault to which I did not have the combination or key. My knowledge was being hidden from me. I couldn't understand why. All I knew was that I didn't have access to the answers I was seeking, and the only way I would get any information was through this strange man. So I decided to make the effort to be nice to him. As my father always said, 'You get more flies with honey than you do with vinegar."

Too bad I was so much better at vinegar.

After what felt like a very uncomfortable and awkward few moments, the man released me from the embrace and offered me his hand with no other explanation.

Out of sheer habit, I took it. I mean, when someone offers you a hand when you're lost and confused while promising you answers, you take it, right?

As I started to follow him, I felt this odd sensation in the middle of my back, right at the base of my ribcage, like Velcro starting to be pulled apart. It wasn't a painful feeling, but it was certainly uncomfortable, and I cried out in agony as the sudden realization of what was happening finally struck me.

My sudden cry gave the man pause and he looked at me strangely, cocking his head to one side as if in an effort to study me from a different angle.

"You felt that?" he asked tenderly, looking at me with compassion and slight intrigue.

"Yes!" I shouted breathlessly. I could feel the tears building up pressure in my eyes as the realization of what was happening continued to wash over me. I had died and this man was escorting me into the afterlife. I wasn't just here for a visit this time. I was here to cross over.

My heart felt as if it were breaking, and my soul began to ache. Even the mist that was surrounding us began darkening in the light.

How could this be? After waiting my whole life to be reunited with Michael as Henry, we were given merely weeks until I was yanked away, back into the all that is, only to be separated from him all over again just as we had come to realize who we were to one another?

It was almost sickening how cruel that was.

God, the pain was unbearable. To think of losing him all over again, after just learning he was, in fact, real and finding ourselves together, in each other's arms, finally reunited...

The ache ripped through my body as if someone were trying to suck out my soul. I guess, in a way, that's what was happening. My soul was beginning to separate from his, as it knew that, without him, it simply could not exist. I may have already been dead, but in this moment, I felt like I was approaching a final death. An absolute death. The death of my very essence. The death of me. The death of my existence. To be forced into the dark abyss of soul separation for all of eternity, never to be whole again, because the piece that was me would be destroyed.

"This can't be happening!" I sobbed as I tried to turn to go back the other way. "I have to get back to Henry!"

"Annalyse, calm down," the man said without loosening his grip. "I understand you're upset, but there is really no need to be so alarmed. You're simply feeling the pull of separation because you still have a karmic connection that has been left unfulfilled. You needn't worry. The two of you will simply come back again in another lifetime to fulfill your karmic debt." As he said this, I realized he was still holding my hand. I only noticed this because his grip tightened on me slightly which caused me to look down at our hands. Noticing, he spoke to me again.

"Come with me and I will explain everything," he continued.

I didn't believe him. I could tell though, that what he was saying he genuinely believed to be the truth. I knew in my soul, though, that it wasn't. I knew there was more going on here. This didn't feel right. If I crossed over, there was no going back. Not this time. That's not how this was supposed to happen. How could he not know this?

As he tried to gently pull me forward more, I could feel the tearing sensation again. Though it wasn't painful in the sense that a human would know and experience pain, the sensation was unbearable. It was like he was trying to pull me away from myself. From everything that made me feel like me, and that's when in hit me.

Oh my God. He is pulling my soul apart!

As if this faceless, nameless, mystery man could hear my thoughts, he looked at me reassuringly and said, "I'm not going to hurt you and you certainly don't have to be afraid. You're exactly where you are meant to be. I'm just here to escort you."

His words were peaceful and soothing as he worked to win me over and to assuage my fears.

The calm, swirling mist that I now realized was, in fact, my actual life essence, comforted me and began to return back to its white coloring. It was the piece of me that was God, the all that is. I could feel the familiarity of creation all around me and I knew this man was telling me the truth. At least what he believed to be his truth. I knew I was safe, and I knew that I was being taken to where my life essence would finally join back with its creator. I could feel the delicious pull, like a bucket of water being pulled back to the ocean, finally rejoining its home. Melting into it, becoming one.

In that moment it almost felt unnatural to be separated from this source. I wanted to be poured back into it and completely assimilate with it. I wanted to be consumed into the warmth, love, and peace that I could feel pulling me, but I couldn't. This wasn't right!

I looked into the eyes of the man who was still holding my hand and I could see love, compassion, and kindness but I also saw something else. Even in this plane my empath superpower was telling me that he didn't feel completely confident in what was happening right now. He was unsure of his position and if what he was doing was the right thing. I knew this too and as much as this felt right, something about it felt very wrong.

I used his uncertainty to my advantage and asked, "Why can I feel you pulling me away? Even with a karmic debt, if it were truly my time, wouldn't I already be separated?" I asked my question with confidence that surprised me.

I didn't even know where this logic came from, but I knew it as truth. I knew I had unfinished business and that it wasn't my time, though part of my soul craved the rest it sensed was just steps away. It was certainly an intoxicating siren song, but I knew that if I followed it, there would be a finality that I wasn't ready for. There was no way I could possibly explain how I knew what I did, but I knew I had something more to do in this lifetime on earth and that if I chose to follow this man, I would forever be changing the trajectory of human kind.

No pressure, right?

The mysterious man looked at me and the emotion of conflict flickered more strongly in his eyes. It was a mixture of fear and understanding. Watching me closely, he tilted his head as if he were some kind of spy who was gathering information through a hidden earpiece before his facial expression shifted from confusion to understanding.

What the hell was going on here?

"Ah..." was all he said as he looked at me with reverence.

He spoke in such a way that sent shivers up my spine and his eyes bore into mine as if he were silently trying to communicate with my soul that was swirling around us. His energy had shifted substantially in just the last few moments. He had gone from uncertainty to being, what I could only describe as being impressed.

What the hell?

Once he got the information he was looking for, he explained, "I understand now. My dear," he began slowly, as if unsure where to start. "You're not feeling your soul pull away from your own host body, the sensation you were feeling was Henry's being pulled out of his."

When he said this, the words washed over me like I had been dunked in ice cold water.

"What!? NO! How can that be?" I shouted at him, "You can't do that!"

"You're right, my dear. I cannot," and with those words he released my hand. "It seems that you have been given a choice."

"A choice? What kind of a choice?" I asked as my mind began spinning, trying to keep up with what I was being told.

"Well, my dear. You have two options. You can either pull Henry's soul back here into the astral plane with you, and you can both step through the veil together to come back again in a future lifetime to be united again in the physical realm to play out your desired experience," he then lifted and parted his hands after his exhaustingly run on sentence, before continuing. "Or you can go back and fulfill your soul contract in this lifetime."

After saying all of this, he simply stood there and continued to stare into my eyes, looking almost impressed by the circumstance, while he silently communicated with some higher part of myself.

The answer seemed obvious, but I felt it was not as simple as it sounded.

"Help me understand. Why are we like this? Why can I not cross over and leave Henry to live out the rest of his life? Why would my crossing over need to result in him dying also? I want to be with him, but I cannot be responsible for his death."

And let's be honest, I also had no genuine interest in having to start over again from scratch in a new life, to feel the pain of the separation through my whole childhood, and be single for who knows how long, until we decided to come together again; especially without knowledge or memory of any of this. Hell-no-thank-you. *It was hard enough the first time. Now that I knew the truth, how could I possibly consider stopping now and starting all over again in a new lifetime to pick up where we left off?*

"Why, not?" the man responded, obviously confused by my logic. "He believed that he was responsible for your death in your previous lifetime together, this is one of the reasons why you agreed to be incarnated this way. So that if you chose to cross over in this moment, he would be forced to come with you. The two of you can never be parted, as you have been bound by The Sacred Magic of Mirrors."

The sacred what?

My mind was spinning.

"I'm sorry, but I still don't understand."

I desired only to be together with Henry. The idea of existing without him, no matter on what plane, reality, or dimension seemed impossible. He was a part of me, and I a part of him. Could I feel this way because of this sacred bond this man was referring to?

The man watched me for a second, as my mind tried to process what he had just shared with me, before responding to me.

"The two of you are unum et anima una," he said, watching me intently.

I simply started at him, while slightly shaking my head and lightly shrugging my shoulders.

"It means, dear one, that you are one soul; One soul that inhabits two physical bodies. Your soul cannot cross over without his because it is the same soul expression. It cannot be separated in such a way after each part has physically incarnated into a body."

I stood there as this truth penetrated every cell in my body. Though I had no actual memory of what he was telling me, I still remembered it. An impossible thing to explain, but it was as if I just knew that this was, in fact, true. We did this so that when I died again, I would have this exact choice. Either cross over with him so that my soul would never need to feel the pain of the separation abyss, or use his soul as a tether to pull mine back through.

God, I wish I could remember why we did this. All I knew to be true in my soul was that I could not cross over. That was not what we had set out to do. There was a purpose to our suffering and I was going to see it through. For us, and for all of humanity.

"I have to return to him." I said to the strange man. "We must finish what we started. He has no debt to pay to me to allow me to take his life in exchange for mine being lost as Sara. I do not hold him to this debt, and I release him from it."

The man started at me with compassion and resignation.

"Then it shall be. The karma will be balanced in another way, for everything must find its equilibrium. It is universal law." He paused for a moment with his eyes closed, and then, opening them, looked right at me and said, "It is done."

Immediately I began to fall backwards as if off the edge of a cliff. In shock, I kept my eyes locked on this man's face as he gave me one last nod of reassurance before the mist enveloped him.

CHAPTER 1
Henry

I felt like my heart was going to burst in my chest, but I kept running.

I ran.

It's all I could think to do, and I had to do something. I ran faster than I had ever run in my life. My muscles burned from the fatigue of having been up all night, but I didn't care. Nothing else mattered except me reaching my destination as quickly as I possibly could. The fire in my burning muscles could have consumed me and I would have still run. Burning alive would have been less pain than the pain I was feeling in my soul and heart. Just thinking about my suffering and anguish caused me to push myself even harder. I welcomed the burning. I was consumed by it, and I welcomed its transformative power. I may as well have been the flame. It was my ally in this moment as it provided the physical pain to numb the emotional pain.

I only had one goal, and nothing would get in my way, not even my tired body; so I kept pushing. Harder. Faster. My breaths huffed and puffed in my chest as my body sprinted down the sterile halls. All I could hear was pounding. My heart fluttered madly as if trying to figure out how to keep doing what it was doing. It was a muscle that I was forcing to work so hard after it had just been broken. Still, I asked it to go. It could not fail me. I could not fail her.

Again….

It was nearly impossible to decipher the difference between my feet falling on the hard floors and my heart beat pounding against my ribcage. It was as if the two things were in complete unison with each other. Each foot fall met with a painful pound of my heart. I was grateful for the noise. It drowned out so much of my mental chatter. Except the one thought cycle I simply could not seem to shake.

Could it be possible?

Could what Annie said be true?

And the most dangerous thought of them all….

Could there still be hope?

I could barely allow myself a scarce thought that could border on optimism, so the thought of having hope, only for it to be dashed away, made my stomach flutter in knots. Hope was dangerous right now. It was such a hazard to my ability to exist in a world without Annalyse that I had not even allowed any thought to enter into my brain that could possibly contradict what I had kenned to be true – what I had seen with my own two eyes.

Annalyse was dead.

The woman whose touch and presence I had craved my whole life was ripped away from me mere weeks after we found each other and reunited. Not only had she been ripped away, but it in the most sickening and gruesome way that would haunt my thoughts for the rest of my life. I shuddered as the images flashed through my head, causing bile to rise into my throat. I almost choked on it due to my labored breaths. Those images flashed through my mind like some macabre light show that had somehow become mingled in with a horror movie that was on the fritz.

After seeing and experiencing what I had, the concept of any form of hope was so foreign to me that I had barely been able to function enough to mentally process what Annie had told me. It was as if my brain was not capable of making such a broad leap from where it was to where Annie was asking me to go.

How could I have not thought about the possibility before?

How could I have forgotten?

Shame and self-condemnation were creeping into the already crowded party of low vibrational thoughts and energies that were jockeying for attention in my chaotic brain. Ironically enough, the demonized hope was the only thing keeping them at bay. Hope was like an angel, shining her light into all the cracks and crevices in my mind, causing all the low energies to scamper off and hide like filthy little cockroaches. It was difficult as is, for hope alone to keep them at bay. It certainly didn't make things any easier that I was afraid to even feed that energy source for fear it might shine light on a truth that I was simply not wanting to have to see or come to terms with.

But I felt like I had no choice.

So, I just kept running.

I had to see for myself.

I had to ken.

It was the only way to give hope the fuel it needed to disintegrate and destroy all the little minions that were running rampant in my head, attempting to claw out, dismantle, and destroy any and all optimism.

The closer I got to my destination the more my heart fluttered and vibrated to the point where I thought it might burst out of my chest.

Until I realized….

These were not regular, nervous butterflies and physical exertion causing this sensation. These were the butterflies that floated through my chest and stomach, as if charged with electricity, that I only felt when I was close to Annalyse. These were *our* butterflies. These were the butterflies that Annalyse and I share together when we feel each other's energy and the butterflies were alive and dancing around in my solar plexus as if in celebration.

And there it was again.

Hope.

Full, unbridled, raw hope.

This could only mean one thing….

If our butterflies were still alive then…. I let my thought drift off without daring to complete it.

But the whisper of the thought was all the fuel I needed to allow this tiny flicker inside me to explode into a volcano of faith and promise that our story may, very well, not be over after it had just barely begun.

My feet slapped against the hard, hospital floors as I practically flew down the halls and tore around the corners until, finally, I could see my destination ahead. I barely slowed as I neared my goal and practically skidded to a stop as I reached the outside of a closed door. Only after triple checking the number on the outside of the door did I slowly push it open, as I tried desperately to slow and catch my breath.

Once I pushed through the door and entered the room, I was immediately surprised by what I saw. There was a woman sitting in a chair, on the far side of the bed where a beautiful, red-haired goddess lay.

Annalyse….

My heart filled with longing at the sight of her.

I'd never kenned her in this form, but this woman was definitely familiar to me. I could feel her energy and recognized it clearly. Even laying on a hospital bed, in a simple gown, with beeping attachments hooked to her, she looked absolutely glorious. I could sense powerful energy radiating from her body as if she was filled with electricity. My soul reacted to the pull of her energy like a moth to a flame. I yearned to be closer. To touch her. To kiss her hand, and let her ken I was there, and that she was safe, and that I wasn't going to let any more harm come to her.

Just looking at her and feeling her energy awakened a carnal need inside me to guard and protect her. The shame of my failure ate away at me like some flesh-eating bacteria. It made me fear I would become some new version of Dorian Gray; that I would appear normal to the outside world, but in reality, be a wrecked and ravaged version of myself. A version who was slowly fading away into dust, being consumed in my own self-hatred due to my own abhorrent failure as a man. I felt as if the only way to absolve myself from this shame would be to protect her from any future harm.

In this moment, as I stared at her beautiful face, I swore to myself that I would do just that.

I barely made a step forward before the seated woman snapped her head up to look at me, obviously startled and feeling defensive. And why wouldn't she be? Here she obviously cared very deeply for her friend and this random, sweaty, beat up man just came busting through the door, panting for breath. I could completely understand her wariness. Her energy very clearly stated that I should not come any closer until she approved, and as much as I could appreciate her solicitousness, I was taken aback by her cat-like response. She was like a lioness, protecting her cub.

"Who are you?" she asked me in a stern tone.

All I could think was, "And who in the hell are *you?*" but I restrained myself. This took considerable effort as I was mentally and physically exhausted and near the end of my tether. At this point, I was functioning solely off of endorphins, testosterone, and the need for my beloved. This combination was quite a toxic and potent tonic. For a moment, I was offended and frustrated by this woman guarding what I felt was mine to keep safe, but it was clear by her behavior that I was not the only one who wanted to guard and protect Annalyse.

I could tell that whoever this woman was, she cared for Annalyse very much. In truth, I had practically forgotten she was there after having become so immersed in my reunion with the love of my soul's existence. I squinted a bit to try to read her expression better, but it was difficult to make out her features, at first. She was sitting with her back to the window, and the morning sun had just started illuminating the outside, making it difficult to see her clearly.

After a few moments of adjusting to the environment, I was able to get a better look at her.

She had long, golden brown hair and golden eyes. After recalling a picture Annalyse had shown me of her with her dearest friend that had been in some of the belongings she had brought back from her apartment when she had picked up Sunshine, I kenned that this young woman must have been her friend Morgan. Annalyse had missed Morgan dearly, and I ken it had been a challenge for her to keep her distance.

Once I realized who this woman was, I thought it would bring Annalyse a level of comfort to ken that Morgan was with her now, but my mind quickly shifted gears as it reeled with how to answer her question.

I figured sticking to the truth was the best course of action. Or at least as close to the truth as possible.

"My name is Henry McLauhlan."

I could see recognition slowly dawn on her face as I said my name. The look was that of shock and confusion. I could easily understand why. I was a relatively well-kenned author in Richmond, and, with some of my books having gone to film, my name was one that was easily recognizable. It would be quite understandable for her to be very confused as to what a married, somewhat-celebrity author, was doing barging into her comatose friend's hospital room in a sweaty frantic.

I paused for a moment as Morgan stared at me. Her eyes trailed over every inch of me and rested on my left hand where my wedding band shined in the morning light, before returning to my face. Self-consciously, I quickly put both of my hands in my front pockets as she stared at me pointedly.

"Annalyse and I…" I tried but embarrassingly trailed off.

I didn't know how to explain what we were. What we are. Fortunately, it didn't seem like I had to.

Morgan looked down at Annalyse's hand which I'd just noticed she had been holding, before saying, "I can tell you care about her very much. She's always been very secretive with her personal life, even with me. I wish she had told me she had been seeing someone."

Her eyes then made their way back to my left hand where it and my wedding ring were hiding. She then took a deep, sad breath before adding, "But I can understand why she didn't. Is that why it took you so long to come see her? Had you not been notified of what happened?"

I wasn't a liar and I hated doing it, but I said, "Aye. Yes. I'd been worried sick about her, but we had recently had a disagreement, so I hadn't been too worried when I didn't hear from her for the first week or two, but then as time went on, I got more and more concerned, so I began making inquiries and that is how I discovered what had happened."

The lie dripped from my mouth like sweet honey, and it surprised me as to how easily it flowed from my lips. Especially, given how ridiculous it sounded that, in today's time it would have taken me two months to learn about someone I loved having been in an accident that resulted in a coma. It felt wrong to hear myself make up such a story to cover the truth of the situation, but what was I to do? Tell her everything and have her have me carted out of here like I was some mad lunatic?

I couldn't risk it. People would never be able to understand the uniqueness of Annalyse's and my connection or relationship. The world wasn't quite ready to open its mind that wide to ken that love could span generations and that the same energy could not be held apart, even by hundreds of years and multiple lifetimes.

"I'm so sorry. Henry, right?" she confirmed. I nodded a response. "I would have contacted you after I found out, but I did not know about the two of you. These last few weeks must have been very difficult for you."

I was surprised at how quickly she bought my story, and I was grateful that at least this was a moment where I could openly speak my truth.

"Aye. Yes. Very much."

I felt uncomfortable thinking that Morgan believed that I had been cheating on my wife with Annalyse, but there was nothing I could say to change that perception of me. I thought it spoke very much to her character that she still treated me with kindness, as someone who loved her friend, instead of with any form of judgment. I could not say I could have extended so much grace if the situation was reversed.

She nodded then said, "I understand."

I believed her.

I could hear the pain in her voice. It was obvious that Morgan cared a great deal for her friend. I assumed it was that pain that was skewing her judgment slightly when it came to believing my flimsy excuse for a two-month absence. As terrible as it was, I was grateful for it, if it provided a smoke screen for my lies. I was so mentally and physically exhausted. I did not ken how I could have kept up a more elaborate charade.

Just as I was struggling between feeling gratitude for her own pain and its ability to disguise my charade, and my disgust with myself that I would use someone's heartache in such a way, Morgan let out a deep sigh and said, "It's my fault that she's here."

I could hear the heartbreak in her words. It was as if every syllable echoed like the sound of a pick striking at an already shattered heart.

I simply stared at her in shock and confusion. I wanted to tell her that she was wrong, and that it was me who was the guilty one. It was I who put her here in the first place, and I who sent her soul to be trapped in some astral abyss that kept her from us both, but before I could begin to try to explain, Morgan did.

"I was the one who convinced her to go out that night, see?" Her words and the longing in her eyes begged me to understand why she felt she must shoulder this burden. "She didn't even want to go. I pushed her into it, but I wanted her to meet someone, actually."

Shaking her head, she scoffed, then continued.

"Now I see why she didn't want to go," clearly implying I was the reason.

She sat with her pain for a moment as a tear made a silent track down the side of her sun-illuminated face, and it was as if the tear itself was creating a new crack in my own, already broken heart.

I wanted to comfort her and tell her she was wrong, but I kenned I could not without revealing too much. So, in this moment, all I could do was honor her and allow her the time she needed to feel through her own self-made suffering as she punished herself with her false beliefs.

Breathing deeply, I just stood there, waiting, until finally she broke the silence again.

"I'm Morgan, by the way," she said, as she wiped her cheek, before returning her attention back to Annalyse.

"It's nice to meet you," I said. "May I?"

Morgan's attention returned to me, briefly, to see that I was asking permission to sit in the chair closest to me that was next to Annalyse's bed and across from where she was sitting.

"Oh, yes. Sure," she responded distractedly before retuning her attention back to Annalyse, again.

Now that we had gotten our strange introduction out of the way, I slowly made my way over to Annalyse's bedside.

This was the first time I had gotten to really see *her* in person and though she was laying on a hospital bed in a boring hospital gown, I could still see her immense beauty. She looked like some sleeping, fairytale princess who was simply waiting for her prince to come along to save her from her cursed slumber with a kiss. Unfortunately for us, I had a feeling that a simple kiss would not be enough to wake my sleeping princess, and I was going to have to figure out another way to help bring her out of her enchanted sleep. It seemed trite to think about her coma being of a magical nature, but, in truth I felt it really was. There was something ethereal going on here that I could not quite grasp or comprehend, but I kenned there was something happening that had absolutely nothing to do with her physical body and everything to do with her soul.

I could feel it.

But what could it be? Had the trauma of what she had experienced been too much for her to want to return to me? Or perhaps, even worse, maybe she did not want to return to me because of my immense failure, as a man, to keep her safe. Could it be possible that she would never be able to forgive me for not being able to save her again; that I would be punished the rest of this life with just the hollow shell of my souls own reflection?

My *neach-gaoil.*

I never could have imagined a greater pain than this. Feeling the longing for someone I never quite kenned truly existed until learning they did, having them at arm's length, and still not really being able to reach them was excruciating. It was the same pain of being in love with a ghost, but even more so because she was right here in front of me. No longer a phantom, but real, yet still unreachable.

I pulled up the chair next to the bed so that I was sitting opposite Morgan and then placed my hand on Annalyse's hand. I had never felt something so delicious in all my life. The surge of energy I felt coursing through my body at our simple touch was enough to send extasy through every cell of my body. The sensation was so powerful, I thought, for a moment, that it could be intense enough to wake her up. Alas that glimmer of hope quickly faded out. Her face stayed the same, as if it were carved from marble by Michelangelo himself.

I took a deep breath in an attempt to soothe my aching soul before returning my attention back to Morgan.

"Can you fill me in on what happened, please?"

Of course, I already kenned what had happened with the accident, but I wanted to ken what happened with her body. What had changed? I worried so that she was in pain in some way, though her body showed no signs of it. I had to ken what was going on now, but in order to get that information I kenned I had to pretend as if I didn't ken anything at all.

She looked up at me with compassion.

"Oh! Of course," she began, almost as if she was embarrassed that she had not offered the information without needing to be prompted. "Annalyse was in a car accident about two months ago. Her injuries had not been too bad, but she fell into a coma. The doctors could not really tell why, and we all assumed that she would simply wake up after some time. It has been weeks, and she is pretty much completely healed, yet she still has not woken up. There has been absolutely no change, until, that is, last night. I had come to visit her once I got off work, and as I was sitting here, I saw a tear run down her cheek. I was absolutely shocked! I ran to get the nurse and she got the doctor, but they could not find anything different. There is still no explanation for why she's not waking up."

I was grateful to her for filling in the story for me, though my heart clenched when Morgan referred to the tear Annalyse shed. I was convinced that the tear had been shed the moment she died. Well, the moment her host body had died. It was due to the tear that Annie had come to tell me about Annalyse. I was ashamed to admit it, but I had completely forgotten that I had asked the kind nurse if she would fill me in if anything changed with Annalyse. This had been before I had kenned who she really was. I had been so filled with guilt about what had happened that I had asked the nurse to keep me informed if her condition changed at all. This was why she had come to tell me about Annalyse after learning that Vivien had died.

The layers of guilt I was feeling in this situation could have stacked up to give Mt. Everest some competition. Through my despair and shock, I had not even remembered that Annalyse's body was still here, in this very hospital, much less considered that she could have returned to it.

When Annie told me that Annalyse's body had registered an emotion, I kenned it in my bones that her spirit had returned to it, though I was terrified to give myself hope for fear I was wrong. My mental and emotional health and stability were on such a thin blade's edge that I could not conceivably allow myself to hope and think that this was indeed a possibility. I only had the confirmation, as I was running down the halls and could feel the familiar electric butterflies flutter in my chest the closer I got to her, that, in fact, her spirit was still here in this physical realm with me.

The most puzzling question now was why couldn't she wake up? It was clear it was not a physical reason, so I kenned it must cause by something happening in the non-physical realm. Something was going on with her soul on an energetic level that was keeping her from being able to wake up.

Our souls were definitely still bound in a union that I possibly will never understand, and I knew, on some level, that hers was destressed. Whether it was by my failure or what happened to her directly, there was some part of her that was not able, or willing to, come back.

I just wished I kenned how to reach her. I would tell her how sorry I was, beg her forgiveness, and vow on my life to protect her above anything else. I didn't care what it took, or how long I had to try, I would find her and bring her back to me. Infinitely.

As I looked at Annalyse's beautiful face and lifted her hand closer to my heart, I spoke silently, "Where are you my *neach-gaoil*?"

I had practically forgotten that Morgan was in the room again, since I had gotten so caught up in my own thoughts, until she reminded me of her presence when she said, "I've been wondering the same thing."

I turned to look at her to see her staring directly at me.

The intensity of her gaze was enough to make me feel uncomfortable.

It was almost as if she were looking for something, and just as I was reaching an extreme level of unease, at the end of her stare, she turned her attention back to Annalyse, to my relief, and said, "I just wish I could go in and get her and show her the way out."

Her words hit me like a waterfall that had just been released from a dam.

"Aye..." I said as I pondered the actual validity of her statement.

Why had I not thought of this before?

Perhaps it was the shock and exhaustion from the last twelve hours. Whatever it was, it washed away with the waterfall that her words had unleashed upon my head.

"Aye," I repeated again as the truth settled over me.

Morgan looked at me bewildered, obviously hoping for more explanation, so I obliged.

"Forgive me," I said as I was now the one who was casting a gaze that was laced with discomfort. I softened my energy before continuing.

"I think you're right, Morgan. Someone needs to go in after her and show her the way out."

I paused for a moment as I turned my gaze back to Annalyse and added, "And I think I ken how."

CHAPTER 2

I felt like I fell forever, or was it for only a moment? Time felt very different here. It was as if everything was happening all at once, yet not really happening at all. Was time even real, or just an illusion?

My fall stopped abruptly, as if I'd suddenly been suspended in a thick gelatin. There had been no impact or jerk from the sudden lack of movement. I simply stopped, suddenly suspended in whatever I was falling through, as if it finally decided to support me.

Flat on my back I quickly opened my eyes, after only just realizing I had closed them, as I felt fluid beginning to surround my body. Due to pure instinct I quickly up-righted myself, looked around, and began treading water. It was in that moment when I noticed a man who was feet from me but submerged under the water.

"Oh my god!" I shouted.

Without hesitation, I dived down under the water and swam towards him. Once I reached him, I wrapped my arms around his legs, as if hugging him, and using what strength I could muster in my legs, lifted him to the surface of the water just before my own head broke the surface.

After a quick assessment, it was easy to see that he appeared to be unconscious. I had no idea how long he had been under water or if he was even still alive.

Dear god.... What the hell had I just fallen into?

Whether or not he was alive, it didn't really matter, I had to try to help him. So, I swam with him over to the edge of the pool. The closer we got to the side, the shallower the water became, as if we had been in some type of lake.

Once I managed to pull him completely out of the water, I rolled him into his side hoping that if he had water in his lungs he would be able to cough it up. The effort of pulling him out of the water had forced me to exert a lot of energy, and my breath heaved as I tried to figure out what my next step was. All I could think was that I had to get the water out of his lungs, so I made my hand into a fist and began hitting his back with the outer edge of my hand in an effort to dislodge any fluid.

Unfortunately, it didn't seem to have any effect, so I rolled him onto his back to begin CPR. It had been years since I had been certified, but I knew the basics and I had to try to help, right? I couldn't just not do anything so I began fumbling around his neck looking for a pulse. My stomach dropped when I couldn't find one. Realizing that that could simply be because I wasn't a medical expert and could totally be prodding his neck in the wrong place, I figured I'd go a different route. I then place my ear on his chest to see if I could hear any breathing or a heartbeat, but there was nothing. There was no life in this man's body.

What the hell kind of place was this that I land in some random lake with a dead guy?

Not knowing what else to do I began chest compressions but just as I began to do so I heard my own voice echo though the cavern that we were in.

"You can't help him."

It was as if it had been my own thought that reverberated throughout the chamber as clear as day. Somehow, I knew this to be true. I also knew in my spirt that he wasn't dead, but there was nothing for me to do for him. He had to be the one to wake up. It had to be his choice. I could not force him to do it. How or why this made sense, I had no explanation, but now that I was no longer operating from a space of pure shock and adrenaline, it was just clear that was what needed to happen.

After trying to position him as comfortably as I could, I started taking in my environment. I sat on my bottom, pulled my knees to my chest, and began looking around. Immediately I noticed that everything was still white, including the long white gown I was wearing.

Well, at least I'm not naked, I thought.

Though this space was still white, it was a very different environment from the one I had just left. The room was like a very large cavern that had been carved out of a gigantic piece of quartz crystal or ice. It was difficult to tell which, but since I wasn't cold and actually quite comfortable, I figured it might have been the crystal option. The walls seemed as if they were self-illuminated in some way, with soft natural light, or perhaps there was light coming in from outside this crystal dome and illuminating it through its semi-transparent walls.

My curiosity was peaked by the strangeness of this place so I decided I would do a little exploration. As I stood up, I gave one last look at the sleeping man lying on the ground next to me.

"I won't leave you or wander too far," I told him. I was uncertain if he could even hear me or why I was even bothering telling this random, maybe even dead, man that I wouldn't leave him or wander too far away from him.

I guess I felt sorry for him, but I had done all I could do at that moment and so at least this way, my hope was that I could find him some type of help. So, I began to make my way around the room. Directly in front of me was a large gold throne that was carved with flowers and adorned with crystals. The seat cushion was royal purple and looked to be velvet.

Fancy, I thought.

To my left there was a long, white table that looked as if it were a gigantic slice of a geode. It reminded me of some epoxy artwork I had seen once at a street faire, where the artist had made the piece look like it was a slice of agate. This had that same feel except it was huge. The table was surrounded by chairs and large enough to seat at least two dozen large people. There was one chair at either end and all along the sides.

I walked past the table and throne to see what looked like a large glass jewelry case. As I got closer to it I noticed that it was full of what looked like other-worldly healing tools. There were large Andara crystals in all different shapes, sizes, and colors. There were crystals that looked like scalpels and there were even other instruments that I could not possibly describe, as if their details were not meant to be shared.

I marveled as I walked the length of the case and reached out to touch the cabinet but stopped immediately. This was the first time I had seen myself since being in this place. My hand looked relatively normal except that it looked like my skin had shimmer in it. It was as if I was glowing and illuminated from the inside.

I held my hand up in front of my face and moved it around so that I could examine it from all angles.

"It's your light body," a voice said from behind me.

I jumped and turned quickly to see....

Wait.

That couldn't be right.

I was looking at *myself*.

What stood before me was a version of myself that I could only describe as Annalyse 2.0. It was me, but… better. It was as if every feature had been turned up and enhanced and made perfect.

"I'm sorry," I began, after the initial shock wore off. "I don't know who you are."

My 2.0 version gave a light laugh that sounded like angelic music before saying, "But of course you do."

Looking at me with a gentle smile she continued.

"I am your higher self," she said before closing her eyes and giving me a small bow of her head. "And these," she continued as she gestured behind her, "are your guides."

To my astonishment there was a crowd standing behind her. I had not noticed that a small group of people had been standing behind her until she pointed them out just now. I use the term people lightly because they were not all human. Two of the creatures looked like a hybrid between a human and a white lion. There was a creature that had a large head with grey skin and what looked like a light blue upside-down triangle on his face. Others looked like regular men and women from all different genres, though mainly ancient times.

I stood there dumbfounded.

"My guides?" I asked in confusion. "Guides for what?"

She looked at me as if the answer was obvious, and, in truth, it kind of pissed me off. I felt like I had gone through the wringer, and, after being tossed here and there in the astral plane, I figured I could be shown a little bit of a break.

Before I could speak again, a man stepped forward from the crowd of what my Higher Self said was my guides and my attention was immediately diverted from my annoyance to shock.

"You!" I said accusingly.

"Yes," the man said with a bow of his head. "It is I."

I looked between him and my higher self accusingly. Did she not know what he just did?

"Galstar has now been appointed as your newest guide after your encounter in the transitory plane," my Higher Self explained.

"Why?" I asked. "He didn't seem to have a clue as to what was going on, and kept trying to force me into transition when I didn't want to go. I wanted to get back to Henry. That's what I chose, but now I'm stuck *here*. Why? Why am I here. Why didn't I wake up?"

Galstar and my Higher Self looked at each other, and it was clear that they were communicating telepathically somehow. This added to my irritation.

"Look, stop with the secrets. I want to know what's going on," I said, slightly louder than I had intended to. As much as I was trying to keep my cool, I was really close to completely losing my shit. Here was this guy, whom I had just left after choosing to come back to Henry, and now he is again in another non-physical space where Henry was not.

Like, seriously, *what the fuck*?

My Higher Self looked at me and said, "We are not keeping secrets. If you cannot hear what we are saying it is because you had chosen not to consciously be included in on those details of your journey. I am your Higher Self, or what some might refer to as your Oversoul. I have knowledge that you do not, in order to guide you along your physical journey. There is much you are not able to understand, due to the low density that is currently on Earth. The information we have does not translate through that density, and, as you are here, represented in your physical mind that operates at that density, there will be some information that will simply not compute."

I stared at her with my mouth opened and my head cocked to one side. I felt like a dog who had just heard a funny noise. The information she just shared with me was the type that makes you feel as if the roof had been blown off of your own head because you realize your whole way of looking at life is wrong and you have to make room for all of the new information. This was the epitome of the sensation "mind blown." Regardless of the struggle I was undergoing, I felt my own cognitive dissonance breaking down and dismantling, and knew she was speaking the truth. There was something in this space that I couldn't explain, but I just *knew* things. Just like with the man who was still lying unconscious next to the pool of water off to the side.

"Annalyse," my Higher Self continued. "You have to trust us. We are here to serve your highest good. Your journey was not one you entered into lightly, and as much as you may think right now that it was simply to reunite with your Henry, it is much, much more than that. Please understand that this journey is not one that can be explained all at once. Because of the density of where you are physically existing, it would be like trying to force all of the contents of an IV bag into your body all at one time. Something like that could kill you. Instead, the fluid has to be slowly delivered, bit by bit, so that your body can receive it, acclimate to it, and then assimilate it into your system. Your physical mind is no different. As much as you can cross through the veil through my mind, *your* mind is still tethered into the physical and will be hindered by that to a degree. That is where we come in." She gestured to all the people and beings in the room.

"We are here to help guide you through your journey so that you can fulfill your soul mission and achieve your destiny."

I let this information sink in while I closed my eyes and took a deep breath.

"Alright," I responded. "I can feel the truth in all of what you are saying, as much as it is a difficult pill to swallow." I paused for a second looking over at Galstar and then back at my Higher Self, then inquired again.

"What can you tell me? Why am I here? Did something go wrong?"

"You're here because you had to die," my Higher Self said.

"Wait. What?!" I said, looking accusingly at Galstar. "You said I wasn't transitioning!"

"Calm down, Annalyse," my Higher Self interjected as I seethed at Galstar. "Just because you died, that does not mean you fully transitioned. Your soul has a duality – the spirit and the soul. The etheric soul, which is the one that is here with us now, and a 'physical soul' or what is referred to as your spirit that becomes energetically attached to the physical body once the etheric soul merges with its energy. Because of this, in order for your ethereal soul to have been released from Vivien's body, her body had to die."

"Ok," I replied as I let this information sink in. "But what about my spirit in *my* body?"

"What about it?" she asked. "It is still in place and since your physical union with Henry it has been calling you back. Didn't you feel the pull?"

"So that's what that was? That's why I was feeling sick in Vivien's body? My own was calling me back?" I asked. "I knew something was going on and that there had been a shift, but I didn't know what was going on."

"Yes, because your etheric soul is the one that is connected to Henry. It created the two physical spirits residing in your body and Henry's body. Your original host body is calling you back so that you can complete your union," my Higher Self continued to explain.

"So, in essence, my soul created a spirit in my body when I was born and it is that spirit that needs to have my soul returned back to it in order to complete my soul's plan? The spirit that was created in Vivien's body was just a temporary tether for me these last few weeks and began failing once it's purpose had been served, since it wasn't an original?"

"Correct. It was a just a temporary means of connection. You will only be able to fully form a soul union with Henry in your own body, and that is needed for what you have chosen to do in this lifetime. For what you both have chosen to do," my Higher Self said.

"And what's that?" I asked apprehensively.

"Come," my Higher Self said as she led me behind the throne.

On the opposite wall of the glass cases that contained the etherical instruments was a large half circle that looked as if it could have been a mirror hanging on the wall, but it was made out of a black rock so nothing reflected off of it. Obsidian maybe?

As I stared at its surface, it was almost as it became fluid, like a thick black oil or hot tar. The sight of it triggered a deep fear within me that it would be poured over my body and suffocate me as it burned. The image of this happening, and the resulting fear that coursed through my body, hit me like an electrical jolt.

I jumped back and quickly looked at my Higher Self for an explanation.

"I'm sorry," she said. Her face looked somber and compassionate. "Those recollections are never easy to reexperience when then creep up from our cellular memories."

We?

"You saw that too?" I asked in astonishment.

She looked at me the way that I look at someone who I think is a complete idiot, but yet seemed to still manage looking kinder than I am sure I ever have in those times, then said, "Of course. I *am* you. We are one and the same, remember?"

Ok, so I deserved the look I got, because that made perfect sense.

"So, you are getting to hear every thought I have?" I asked, feeling slightly embarrassed and also kind of like a kid knowing they can get under their caretaker's skin and liking it.

"Yes, Annalyse. Everything." It was clear she was not amused by my decline into immaturity.

I considered this information for a moment and then I had a realization that answered so many questions I have had in the past.

"Is that where the random 'thoughts' I have, that seem to come out of nowhere, come from? Are those *your* thoughts?"

"Yes," my Higher Self responded. "Most of the time. This is typically what people refer to as channeling. It's really just tunning into your higher self and allowing that part of you to bypass your ego, which would work as a filter."

Interesting.

I had heard of people channeling other "beings" before. I guess, in some cases, the "other being" is actually the part of them that is still on the other side of the veil.

"You said most of the time," I continued. "Who else would be putting thoughts into my head."

"Sometimes it could be one of your guides or an angel giving you guidance. Or it could be Henry as you two have a telepathic connection with each other."

"Wait! What?" I said in utter shock. "We do? How?"

"Since your souls are connected, you can communicate to each other through that tether."

"Does that mean I could get him a message now? Tell him where I am?" I asked hopefully.

"I am not sure it would do any good Annalyse. Henry is in a very low vibrational state right now. In order to receive a communication from you like that, he would need to be tapped into the highest vibration that exists, which is love. Currently, though he is fueled by his love for you, he is not in that emotional state. Like energy attracts like energy. Remember this."

Hearing about Henry's pain broke my heart. As the anguish came over me, I could see that the black tar like substance began to move and change, and I felt the need to walk towards it, to examine it more closely. Without even thinking, I was compelled to reach out my hand to touch the moving liquid which was mesmerizing, though a part of me was uncertain of this decision. I ignored that part of me, and as my hand made contact with the surface, I was instantly sucked through.

As I passed through the portal, I heard my Higher Self in my head.

I am sorry Annalyse, you needed to get into the same vibration of what you must witness, or at least as close to it as possible, in order for it to not destroy you. Like energy attracts like, so you had to be closer to that vibration.

Not destroy me?

Oh, great. This sounds like it is going to be really fun.

CHAPTER 3

I came out on the other side onto what looked like barren ground. Everything seemed red and dry, if the planet was dying. It made me think of what it would be like to be on planet Mars, but instead of seeming like a cool adventure to a new planet, it felt sad. Something terrible had happened here. I could tell that things once were beautiful and lush, but something that was clearly a cataclysmic event had happened to drain the life out of the planet.

What happened here? I thought, as I looked around at the desolation.

Even the sky looked red.

At least, all but a section far off to the left. This part was grey, almost black, and it was undulating with an intensity that made my body fill with anxiety, as if I could feel the unstable, chaotic energy writhing within my very cells. It appeared as if this part of the sky was a massive storm approaching. There was so much electromagnetic energy pulsating through the black clouds that I began to hear its electrical hum, even with it being at such a great distance. As I watched the storm clouds rumble and churn with their ferocity, something in me knew that this storm in the distance would not remain distant for much longer, so I began to make my way in the direction I felt led to go.

I saw a path ahead of me that lead up a rocky mountainside, so I began making my way towards it. The path clearly had been a landmark that had gotten a lot of use at one time, as it was clearly etched into the mountain, almost as if it had been chiseled there by every foot-fall that had landed on it. As steep as the climb was, I did not feel tired or out of breath as I made my way to my guided destination. There was no need to rest or catch my breath. I simply climbed.

Eventually I made my way to the top of the mountain. From this vantage point, it seemed as if I could see for hundreds of miles, and, from where I stood, I could only see death, decay, and a barren wasteland. As I looked around, I started remembering this place and how it once used to be. Lush, thriving, green and beautiful. Teaming with life and vitality. This was somewhere I once lived.

Somewhere I had once called home.

It pained my soul to see my home in such destruction and desolation, but I knew that this was why I was here. This was what I had to do. What I came here to do. I remembered why I was to come to this place. I stood on the mountain and rooted myself there as I spread my arms out wide. As I did so, I got a glimpse of my hands, and I noticed that they were a greyish blue and I only had three long fingers. I was not sure who I was in this time or place, but it was clear that I was not human.

As my arms stretched open wide, I tilted my head back and looked up at the sky again. I could see the storm approaching as I accepted my role as the sacrificial lamb to give us another chance. Another opportunity. My planet and race had ended. We had failed, and now something that was once full of life, was only but a carcass, cast aside after it had been robbed of its life force. This was the only way for us to try again. It was now time to start something new and I would be the one to help create it.

May we do better this time, I thought. *Let it all be worth it. Let us find redemption. Let us find ourselves and remember who we are.*

The storm was now undulating directly overhead.

It was upon me and it raged like a demon out of hell coming to collect its payment for the sins of an entire species. I stared at it as it consumed me, hoping I would satisfy the debt.

The last thing I saw was a massive electrical surge as the cloud harnessed its energy, and then a blinding flash as an unmeasurable amount of electricity hit my body with enough force to split me in two.

Suddenly I was back in front of the black wall of fluid-like substance, and I jerked my hand back from its surface as quickly as if it had burned me. I turned to stare at the group of individuals behind me with a look of shock on my face. I then scanned the crowd for one guide in particular until I found the large grey head with the blue, upside-down triangle on its face. I looked down at the creature's hands, recognizing them as the same I had just had. The Being simply stared at me as I stared at it, while I tried to make sense of what I had just witnessed. What I had just experienced.

"Tell us what you saw," my Higher Self spoke as she stepped forward.

"Why?" I said in frustration.

Good lord!

I had just experienced a very confusing, heartbreaking, and traumatic incident and here this *Being* who is supposed to know everything in my head, is just wanting me to immediately regurgitate it like some bad sushi I had picked up at a gas station?

"If you see everything I do, hear everything I think, and experience everything I do, why do I need to tell you what I saw?" I snapped back at her. "After what I just experienced, I feel like *you* should be explaining to *me* what I saw, not the other way around."

My Higher Self looked at me and sighed before explaining.

"You need to tell us because what you witnessed has been a repressed collective wound since the inception of the human race. This wound has been so deeply hidden that you agreed to incarnate into this life experience, die twice, have your divine feminine energy attacked and stolen, and many other things that many others could not bear the weight of carrying, in order to set about a cascade of events that would lead you here and into the moment we have been waiting a millennia for – so that you could cross through the Black Veil of The

Collective's Shadow in order to retrieve it. This is a memory that has been hidden from all of us, and it is time to begin the process of healing it. It was this that started it all. That caused the creation of the Witch's Wound that is carried by both women and men alike. In order to heal it, we must understand where it came from. We need to know it's origination story."

I looked at her and then back at the Being with the upside-down triangle on its face and said, "Why don't you ask him?" while jerking my chin in his direction.

"You know what I saw, don't you?" I asked him in a more compassionate tone.

"Yes," my Higher Self said.

I whipped my head back in her direction, giving her my full attention again.

"But," she continued. "He is not able to speak what needs to be said as he does not communicate in the required way, and the activation must be spoken out loud by the one who received it."

I stared at my Higher Self as I took some deep breaths, waiting to get out of my mind and into my truth so I could feel into whether her words resonated with me. After a moment or two I could feel their validity.

I turned my attention back to the grey Being.

"So, you saw it too?"

He merely stared at me. As he gazed into my eyes, I could feel a rush of warmth spread through my body as if some type of alchemizing agent had just been released from every cell. Then, as if something else had overcome me, I began speaking directly to the grey Being.

The words came out as if I were speaking some type of poetry. A love story, written from a broken heart.

"I had a dream about you and me. We were a large, beautiful tree. A tree of life. The Tree of Life. We were massive, strong, and so intertwined in each other's energies that you could not tell one from the other. We were once the same and it was just us.

Do you remember?

Then the lightning struck, and we were torn apart. Both halves of the tree falling away from each other, turning black and unyielding of the fruit we were designed to make. You going left and me going right. We crashed onto the broken earth like a canon blast. Or was that the sound of my heart breaking? Our heart breaking.

Did you hear it too?

We searched for one another. Looking. Seeking. Growing our branches as they stretched across the barren wasteland. At last, we found each other, but we didn't recognize the other. Our branches simply grew and raged against one another. We were fighting each other.

Could you feel it?

The pain was unbearable. You tried to swallow me up and overtake me. You tortured and oppressed me, fearing my growth. Our growth. You tried to destroy me and sometimes you succeeded. This destroyed us both for your war on me was a war on you, as we were both the same.

Are both the same.

Then, the fire came. It shot from the earth at the space where we were torn apart. It healed us. It raged a tower-like inferno that rained down its purification and cleansing. The earth began to wake up. Turning green and blue with life. Breathing remembrance into our branches.

Don't I know you?

Finally, from this Flame was born a new tree. A small tree, but a strong tree, and we became its roots. Its heritage. Its lineage. Its memories. We became the new tree. Finally, we found each other again. We are now returned to our true nature.

Why can't you remember?

Wake up, beloved. There is much work to do. The roots are whispering to me. Hear, listen, remember. I am tired of fighting. I surrender my will to try to make you be anything other than what you were meant to be. I do not know what more to do.

So, I am just going to love you."

Once I finished speaking, the words rang out in the cavern like a haunting refrain.

As I had been relaying this message, I had watched the Being I was speaking to and I had witnessed it shift. The triangle on its face darkening until it was almost completely black. I somehow knew that this was its way, once our way, of expressing sorrow instead of crying as humans do.

My heart ached for this creature. I could feel its sadness and pain. The separation it felt with its own self was a pain I knew all too well. It was a pain I had lived with my entire life. The best way I could describe the pain would be to say it was that of death. The true loss of someone you held dear, but in this case that someone was you. It was as if a part of this Being had died, and in truth, a part of him had died, and a part of me *had* died too. A part of all of us had died. And we all felt the pain, though we never understood it, or knew what it was. It was the war we waged against each other not realizing that it was a war we waged only on our self.

For thousands of years we had been asleep, with our eyes closed, and every time a new branch reached out to us we tried to destroy it for fear of not understanding what it was. All this time, we were simply destroying parts of ourselves. Fighting against parts that went against what we knew to be true in our limited field of knowledge. Now our eyes are opening, and we have begun to see what we have done.

This knowledge suddenly sinking onto our shoulders like a heavy burden to bare. This is a deep pain and reflects the famous words of Jesus, "Forgive them Father. They know not what they have done." How could we? It would be like breaking something while sleepwalking. How could we possibly have known? We simply did not.

I could see now that the first step in the process of what we were putting into motion was forgiveness. Forgiveness of ourselves and that of others for the role we played in these atrocities on our fellow brothers and sisters in humanity.

I approached the being and reached out my hands to it.

"I am Ky," I heard him communicate telepathically to me once our hands connected.

"Ky, did we once know each other?" I asked.

"We are one another," was the response.

This statement did not make sense to me. It seemed too cryptic and unclear. How could we be the same? We were nothing alike.

"Help me understand," I communicated.

Ky looked me deeply in the eyes and spoke, *"I am a physical representation of the consciousness we once shared. Both male and female existed together as one, in one body. When our home was destroyed, we were split into two parts in order to give new life to a New Earth for there was no one left to mate with, so we sought the most intimate relationship of all: one with our own self. In the search for each other the masculine, so driven with need to be with the feminine, tried to take and consume her.*

For thousands of years the masculine oppressed and abused the feminine in an attempt to reclaim her, not understanding that they had no claim; she was already him and he was her. You cannot take from yourself to give to yourself. This is impossible. This was how they tried to cope with their pain.

Over the years and generations, as they learned their efforts did not satiate their need, they then condemned women as something to tempt them, demonizing them by saying they were something to be feared.

The masculine felt the need for the feminine but taking them did not bring them the satisfaction they so longed for, so they attempted to control woman instead, thinking this would somehow bring them peace. It did not. It only fueled war, pain, and suffering. This evolution has spanned for thousands of years and many soul cycles of healing.

Finally, it is time for the reunion of the soul. Many men feel this shift happening and they fear it, because of the imbalance that has been in place for so many soul cycles. But there is no reason to fear the falling away of the old, broken paradigm, as the new takes its place. The rise of the feminine does not mean the fall of man, it instead brings more power to all. It brings wholeness and oneness. It brings healing and balance. The world is finally ready for this to begin."

At no point did he disconnect his eyes from mine as he communicated to me. The intimacy between us on a soul level, with the depth of this connection and communication, was that which I had only experienced with one other person.

Henry.

It was in this moment that I understood and began to remember. In the current lifetime I was experiencing, Henry and I were the physical embodiments of the Being that had been split in two to give birth to a new humanity. We had needed the separation to create contrast for growth and evolution. As the universe is constantly expanding, there was a need to split off one of the already evolved factions, just like a river splitting into two separate streams. This was necessary for the expansion of the universe because through the contrast there was the ability to desire more and through that desire, more was created. Our species, the Drakna, were chosen for this task because through our failure to grow and evolve, we killed our own planet. Once our consciousnesses split, the planet was restored, and the human race began.

Knowing my Higher Self was able to take in all this information that I had just recited in my head, I turned to her and asked, "Is this why, in the beginning, our creative energy, or what people see as 'God,' was so fearful about us tapping into and recognizing our separation or seeing that we were different? For fear that once our eyes were opened to the truth that we would destroy ourselves once again?"

"Yes…" she said with a small nod, confirming my theory. "It wasn't until the Kundalini energy could no longer be bound, that it began to rise, waking up each Chakra center and activating the unique divinity in each, that their eyes became opened, and they realized that they were different. It's not a coincidence that Kundalini energy is associated with snakes. All stories have *some* truth to them."

She sighed heavily, as if overwhelmed with sorrow then explained.

"It's ironic," she said. "It was through our own awakening into our humanity that we began to see each other as enemies, and it is the same energy that awakens those today so that they remember that we are all one."

I nodded in recognition of how ironic it can be that the thing we create as our salvation must sometimes first be our undoing.

Now that Ky's story and my reactivated memories had filled in the gaps, I knew what more I needed to do here in this space with my work with Ky, so I turned my attention back to him.

"Thank you for explaining, Ky. I understand now." I said, then added, *"And thank you for your part in this journey and our mission together."*

I then stepped forward and embraced him while whispering aloud, *"And I forgive you."*

I granted him this forgiveness as I recognized that he represented the masculine energy of the Being that we both once were. The healing would be able to start once I forgave myself, and Ky provided me with a physical representation of the version of myself that I needed to grant forgiveness to.

I pulled away from the embrace and locked eyes with Ky for a few moments. He then closed his eyes for a long, slow blink, almost as if he was relaying or interpreting a message, and, upon opening them, added one last thing.

"We have heard your cry, and we are ready to answer. Thank you for your sacrifice, Mascarnum. It is now time I make mine."

And with that, he dissolved into golden-white dust right before my eyes.

I stood frozen as I stared at the shimmering powder left in my open palms where his hands had been resting just moment before.

It looked like it could have been stardust.

And at almost the exact same moment that he disappeared; a loud gasp rang through the cavern

71

pulling my attention away from my recently disembarked friend.

I whipped my head around to find where the sound came from only to see that the man who had been lying on the ground by the edge of the pool had just woken up.

CHAPTER 4

Henry

"Shannon, I need your help," I spoke frantically into my cell phone as I paced back and forth in the chilly November morning air.

"Henry?" I heard on the other end of the line, "Tell me what's going on."

Shannon sounded tired, as if I had woken her. I had been so distracted by what was going on that I had not even paid attention to the time. I took a look at my watch to see that it was just past seven in the morning. Part of me felt bad for waking Shannon up so early, but the other part – that was so determined to get Annalyse back – was simply grateful that she had cared enough to answer the phone at such an early time.

"Where to begin?" I replied as I ran my hand through my messy, dirty hair while pacing back and forth.

"Well, I've always found that the beginning is helpful," she said groggily.

Some would have thought that she was being a bit sarcastic with this statement, but I kenned her well enough to ken that her statement was not meant at all that way.

"I need to know everything if I'm going to be able to help."

I looked around the grounds to confirm that I was indeed alone and that no one could overhear our conversation before responding. The last thing I needed was some hospital staff member overhearing my conversation and thinking I had lost it and was having some kind of mental fit or something.

"Shannon, I hardly know where to begin. It sounds so crazy."

"Henry, you know as well as I do that crazy is only a term to represent something that the average person cannot understand because they cannot make sense of it in their limited 3D way of thinking. I am not average, one, and two, I love learning more and more about how much more expansive our reality is than what I am currently aware of. You were guided to me to help you for a reason. Let me do it."

"Aye," I replied. She spoke the truth, and this was exactly why I kenned to reach out to her about what was going on. She was the only one I kenned who could possibly even come close to understanding Annalyse's and my connection and what was happening between us now, so I decided the best thing in this moment was to tell her everything, and I did.

I told her about the car accident and how Vivien had died and Annalyse had woken up in her body. I explained how it took us time to understand what had happened and why and how we had discovered that we had been the two souls from the past life memories we had both been haunted by our entire lives. I even told her about the night that we physically connected and how it was more than as if we were simply making love, but that love was making us.

The words spilled out of me like sand through my fingertips. Even if I had wanted to hold onto the words it was completely impossible at that point. I had taken the lid off a pot that was boiling under so much pressure that there was no stopping the force behind it.

It was not until I got to what happened last night that my words began to stick in my throat, like a lump being formed in an effort to keep down the bile that I could feel attempting to rise into my mouth. After several deep breaths, and trying to remain as detached from what I witnessed happen to Annalyse in an effort to not retraumatize myself, I felt that I could share with Shannon what happened without breaking into utter hysterics.

Once I was able to continue, I communicated the absolute bare minimum about what Annalyse had endured when her soul was still inhabiting Vivien's body, while carefully maneuvering myself through that emotional minefield. Finally, I was able to explain to her that I could feel that Annalyse's soul had returned to her body, but she seemed to be stuck in the astral realm, for some reason, and this was why I needed her help.

In truth, I would not ken anyone else to ask. I did not see it as a coincidence that she and I had met previously and that she had helped me understand about these types of things. The more I thought about it, the more I came to believe that Shannon and I must also have a soul contract with one another, and a main part of that contract was for her to help me along my path with Annalyse. I was grateful to have access to her.

This was a very lonely journey that Annalyse and I had chosen for ourselves, and I would stop at nothing to be reunited with her again in the physical. What Annalyse had not realized through our journey was that, in a way, I too was going through a sort of living state of comatose. It was as if I was only living a half-life, and it was not until she reentered my experience that I truly began to live. I wanted to give that gift back to her, so I was determined to help her reawaken so that we could finally have the life together that was so cruelly stolen from us all those years ago.

Just as she had brought me back to life, I would bring her back to life.

Shannon had listened to my story the entire time I spoke, not once making an interjection or query, and, even after I finished speaking, she still remained quiet for a few moments.   I waited patiently for her response as my stomach tightened under the worry that she may, in fact, not be ready for this much "expansion."

Just as I started wondering if perhaps our call had been cut off, I heard Shannon's voice come through the speaker.

"Henry," she spoke very slowly and calmly. "At what hospital are you?"

I was very confused by her question. It was probably the last thing I would have expected her to say, but I still answered.

Her reply took me off guard as much as her previous question had.

"Stay where you are and text me her room number. I'm on my way."

And she was gone.

I stared at my phone for a moment in disbelief. What did Shannon ken that she was not telling me? What was so significant to her that she would get herself out of bed and rush to see me and my comatose lover at the crack of dawn?

I typed up the text to Shannon as quickly as I could and noticed that my hands were becoming shaky. This was no doubt due to the exhaustion that was slowly trying to wash over me like a tidal wave that wanted to swallow me up, on behalf of the ocean, to be pulled down into her depths.

I hit send, and my stomach knotted as I was becoming more keenly aware of the fact that I could not stave off this pull to sleep that felt like an Angel of Death attempting to carry me adrift. I kenned I needed to rest, and soon, but how? How could I possibly sleep when Annalyse was stuck somewhere in the astral plane? Not only could I not rest because of the guilt I would feel not doing anything to help her, but my arms would ache not to hold her near me as we were intertwined in each others energy and body, like we were meant to be.

This whole situation felt like some nightmarish version of some fairytale where I was some prince that could not wake his beloved from her cursed slumber. It was utter agony to have been so close to being back in union with my Anam Faileas only for her to have been ripped away so quickly. And the feeling of having absolutely no control made it so much worse. Within one twenty-four hour time span, I felt like every ounce of manhood had been ripped from me.

I could not protect my beloved from one of the most atrocious acts that could be committed by one person to another, and now I just have to sit by powerlessly as I surrender her to whatever she may be experiencing in the astral plane. This made my own mind begin to spin and reel. I kenned how it was all too easy to cause ourselves suffering by being stuck in our own mind because I was doing that very thing to myself in that moment.

My thoughts went to the absolute darkest possibilities that it could have. What was Annalyse witnessing? What was she experiencing? Was she having to relive what happened to her last night?

Was she reliving the pain of our separation from the lifetime that we both have memories from? Was something keeping her trapped in whatever space she was in?

I felt so unmatched for this battle. Even as a warrior, I felt so underprepared and under-armed for the fight I was up against. How do you fight an invisible enemy? How do you enter a battle where you do not have access to the place the war is being waged?

I slowly made my way back up to Annalyse's hospital room. Morgan looked relieved to see me when I entered. This immediately sent a jolt of panic though me.

"Morgan, is everything alright with Annalyse?" I asked quickly.

"Oh, yes. Nothing has changed. I was just needing to head out and was hoping you would return before I left."

"Ah," I responded. "May I give you my mobile in case you get any updates, and can I have yours in case something changes while I am here?"

"That's a good idea," she said as she fumbled in her bag to find her cellular.

I could tell she was most likely about as tired as I was. After exchanging numbers, I wished her a safe journey home and assured her I would let her know if there was any change. Just as she was walking out the door she turned back to ask, "Did you reach your friend? The one who you think could help?"

"Aye," I said with a nod. "She's actually on her way here now."

Morgan looked surprised by this comment.

"Wow, she must be a good friend," she said.

"Aye," I said again. "I think she wants to see her in person."

I honestly was not clear on why Shannon needed to see Annalyse in person. What good would it do to see a stranger lying asleep on a bed?

"I guess that makes sense."

I guessed so too…. But what did I ken in this moment? I was completely dead on my feet.

As Morgan turned to continue out the door, she paused once more to look back at me.

"Henry, be careful. I know you're wanting to go in to find her, but don't you get lost too. The mind is a tricky place. I've been thinking about this while you were outside talking to your friend, and the truth is, she may not even realize she's there. She may not even know you or remember who you are.

Where she is, you could be an enemy or a stranger to her.

We have to recognize the fact that there is a reason she hasn't come back, but we can't ignore that we don't know what that reason is. Please just be careful that you don't add to it. I know you mean well, but sometimes we want to help people because we are actually wanting to assert our will over another, hoping for a certain outcome, instead of allowing them their journey and simply supporting them through it."

She paused briefly again, as if trying to figure out if her words were reaching me, then added, "Henry, I just caution you to check your motives before taking any action."

I watched her in surprise as she turned and walked out the door.

My utter exhaustion was making it very difficult to process what she had said to me. It was as if the gears in my head were all stuck and mucked up with something sticky. My mind was processing things very slowly, and it was if things were starting to move in slow motion. I could feel a strong pull to be next to Annalyse, and I needed to rest in some capacity, so I made my way back over to the chair I had been inhabiting before I had gone to the parking lot to contact Shannon in hopes that she would be able to aide me in my journey to bringing Annalyse back to me.

After sitting down in the chair next to Annalyse's bed, I did my best to meditate on Morgan's words as I held Annalyse's hand and gently made circles on the back of it with my thumb.

As much as I loathed to admit it, Morgan had a point. Of course, I wanted to help Annalyse, but I had to do it from a space of being in service to her, not service to myself. Why was that so difficult to navigate? I think the hardest part about that is to tell the difference. We can so easily convince ourselves that we know what's best for someone else; all the while it's just our ego trying to assert control over a situation because we are operating from a place of fear instead of love.

Or was it because I wanted to believe so badly that she and I both wanted the same thing?

"Christ." I said under my breath.

The pain it brought upon me just to flirt with the idea that Annalyse was staying away from me because she wanted to was like an axe in my chest. But, how could I blame her, eh? I failed her. I couldn't protect her or save her and she died, because of me. This would be something I would have to live with my entire life. A debt I would always be needing to pay.

I would have gladly given my life to save hers, but part of me was grateful for how the circumstances were in this moment, as I truly hoped that wherever Annalyse was, she was at peace and felt safe and cared for. Annalyse had suffered enough, and the idea of her being in the level of pain I was in now, pained me as much as my being in this situation did. If one of us was to suffer from the loss of the other, I would carry that burden for her, as she had already carried it several hundred years ago.

Maybe this was my karma.

My punishment.

I just hoped that I was strong enough to withstand it.

As much as I wanted to make sure I was doing everything I could for Annalyse because it was what she needed, I kenned that it would take extra effort and care for me to make sure I was mindful of my motives. I wanted so badly to make things right, but I had to remember that making them right could look very different to many people. It was certainly a confusing and complicated arena for me to try to navigate within. Making things right, justice, and revenge all could feel very similar but were actually *very* different. I kenned I would have to be mindful of what energy I was working from.

Staying in a space of service to my beloved would be my best course of action as I navigated this emotional tempest.

I looked at Annalyse's peaceful, sleeping face and whispered, "Tell me what you need, Anam Faileas."

I then allowed my head to rest back on the chair and closed my eyes as I continued rubbing the back of her hand with my thumb.

CHAPTER 5

I turned quickly to look at my Higher Self.

"What just happened?" I asked in shock.

She looked from me to the man who was now sitting up at the edge of the pool and back to me again before responding.

"You went through the Barnium Portal to re-experience a past-life memory. That's why you are here. The safest way for your mind to have been able to process the information was to do it here, in the Iserus Chamber. If this memory had resurfaced while you had been fully present in your physical form, it would have shattered your psyche. This memory had been so suppressed, due to the level of trauma your soul had experienced by it, that it has taken millennia worth of lifetimes of healing to be able to retrieve it. This memory was that of the origination of the Mirror Souls. We have been waiting a very long time for you to be able to retrieve it so that you would be able to speak the incantation over Ky to activate him."

What. The. Fuck.

My mind was reeling, and I began pacing around as the information marinated inside my head. This information was a lot to process. More so than the memory itself. I guess I had chosen the right way and time to access it because, as much as I found it sad, I truly had no other attachment to it. The difficult part was wrapping my mind around the idea that my soul expression had been one that had experienced the decimation of its kind and had its soul ripped apart into — what had she called it — Mirror Souls?

I thought for a second about this term before being able to access the memory, then I turned to look at my Higher Self.

"'Anam faileas?' This is what Henry calls me. He said it means 'Soul Reflection.' A mirrored soul?"

My Higher Self simply stared at me as if waiting for me to answer my own question.

Since I got no answer, I asked another question, "And what does '*Mascarnum*' mean?"

"Ky was speaking to you in the language you shared before your soul was split. *Mascarnum* means Divine Creator. He was acknowledging the part of your being that is what you would know as God. Think of the term as the equivalent of when someone say's 'Namaste' but instead of saying you are honoring that person's soul, to refer to them as *Mascarnum* would be as if you were directly addressing it."

Wow.

So, Ky literally was addressing my soul as if he were speaking directly to the piece of the Divine Creator that resided in me. In essence, by referring to *me* as *Mascarnum,* he was saying that I was that very energy, the energy of Divine Creation.

So, where did Henry come into play in all this?

"I don't understand then," I began. "If Henry is my Mirror Soul, then who was Ky? Who is that man?" I indicated the man who now happened to be making his way over to us.

"How can Ky, or this man," who was now standing with us, "be my Mirror Soul if Henry already is?"

"Annalyse, who am I to you?" my Higher Self said to me.

"My Over Soul. That is what you told me," I responded.

"Have you not looked at this man you so valiantly tried to rescue from the Iserus?" she asked motioning towards him.

Actually, I had not. I had been so caught up with trying to save him and trying to process everything that was happening, I had not paid much mind to what he looked like. I turned my head to look at him and gasped as I took several steps back.

"Henry?"

The man smiled at me and replied in a heavily Americanized Scottish accent, "I am Ky. I am Henry's Higher Self, or as you just described, his Over Soul."

Holy shit.

"So why were you in the pool of water?" I asked as I used my hand to motion in the direction of the pool I had discovered him in.

He smiled again, and spoke to me almost as a loving father would to his child saying, "The Iserus is a type of incubation chamber. It is where your soul resides until the physical spirit is ready for its Light Activation – or what you would ken as a Spiritual Awakening.

The soul enters the Iserus when the spirit experiences its trigger circumstance or experience in the physical world that would activate the need

90

for the integration of the soul and the spirit. The soul remains in the Iserus until the physical body is ready to receive the connection. This can be a very challenging experience for many and is what is referred to as the Dark Night of the Soul. It is during the time that the soul is incubating and working to connect with the spirit that people begin questioning so many things about their lives, begin awakening to new truths and awareness's about themselves or the world, and have whole believe systems shattered. Depending on how developed their ego became in their physical lifetime, this can cause a very emotional and painful experience because there is so much resistance. The soul is designed to connect with the spirit in this union called Carthesis so that one can fully align with their Higher Self and have a complete connection with the Divine."

I had so many thoughts running through my head as I processed this information, but one stuck out the most.

"I do not understand. If the soul enters into the Iserus when the trigger happens, and then comes out when the Spiritual Awakening begins, why wasn't my Higher Self in the pool with you and me when I got here?"

Ky looked at me with a tilted head, "Wasn't she?"

I thought for a moment then turned to look at my Higher Self. She must have heard the question formed in my mind because she answered it without me having to ask.

"Yes," she said. "I had been in the Iserus when you joined us here. It was when you woke up that I woke up also. You just did not notice my presence until I addressed you directly, because you had been so distracted trying to 'save' Ky."

"I don't understand," I said. "How can you be my Over Soul if you are unconscious in a pool of gelatinous water? Are you supposed to support and guide me? How can you do that while you are asleep?"

Ky laughed at my question, and it made my stomach flip to hear such a jubilant sound escape from this man who sounded just like Henry. I just stared at him, trying to hide the longing I felt build up in my body while also trying to ignore the embarrassment I felt knowing my own Higher Self was probably very aware of the desire I was feeling.

"I love your terminology!" Ky said light heartedly. He was a very stark contrast from my own Higher Self. As much as I enjoyed that, I was not sure how much I loved how uptight my own Over Soul was.

"Dear Annalyse," he continued. "We are not unconscious in that state at all. We are integrating with the Spirit that lives inside our human bodies. If anything, our consciousness here on this side of the veil is far more accessible while we are in the Iserus, though it feels the opposite in the human body because there is a perceived feeling of losing one's self during this process. This is not caused by separation from the Soul, but separation of the ego, which is only a physical construct. The integration process overrides the ego, and some egos have grown very large and strong pain-body thoughtforms that do not want to release their captive. It can be a very difficult struggle for some because the thoughtform creates a false narrative that the falling away of the false identity they hold onto will be their undoing, when in fact it is only the thoughtform's undoing. But it has worked to convince the mind that they are one and the same. This creates much unnecessary suffering that can drag out for years or the rest of someone's physical lifetime. It is in the surrender where the relief is found."

I thought about what he said for a moment. I could connect with his point. I had seen this first-hand with acquaintances. Something drastic had happened in their life that became a pivotal moment. It either seemed to have broken them, or for others, it catapulted them into a new direction in their life where it seemed so obvious they were meant to be there that anything else in their past was just a warm-up preparing them for this season of their life.

"Ky?" I asked. "If you only enter the Iserus when we are ready for our Awakening, what is your role before this?"

"Before integration through the Iserus, we can only act as an observer and communicate through synchronicities, signs, symbols, and messages from others who have already integrated with their own Over Soul. Or as you would call it, those who have spiritually awakened. Once we have fully integrated, we are able to watch over you *and* communicate with you directly."

"Who is watching over us while you are in the Iserus?" I asked. "That seems scary to think you have been watching out for us and then stop. Especially, like you said, for what could be years."

"Well, you see, time works very differently here. For the body it may be years worth of physical plane experience, but here it is mere moments.

"What happens if someone never fully integrated and does not awaken before they die?"

"They join us here after crossing over. Much like you did. But instead of crossing over, you came here through a more temporary process so that you could retrieve the lost memory for the collective."

"Why could I have not just done that between a lifetime, if I come here after each one?"

"Because when you incarnate you do not take conscious memories with you and this was something you would need a conscious memory of. Yes, all memories are stored in your brain and even every cell in your body, and you have access to all of your lifetimes worth of memories through your spirit that is physically integrated with your cells. But these are all stored in the unconscious brain; you do not have direct access to them. They exist there to form your reality as a lens that filters information to make it align with your unconscious programming that has been created from lifetimes worth of experiences. This is how people feel and are aware of their Witch's Wound. At an unconscious level, they still remember what happened to them when someone feared their gifts and found them to be too dangerous to coexist in society."

I scoffed at his wording. "Too dangerous to coexist in society" was a very polite way of saying that people, and mostly men at that, brutally murdered almost five million women in a three-hundred-year period of time simply because they were different, while men who practiced the same arts were revered as scientists, physicians, and scholars. I could feel the heat build in my body thinking of the flashes of memories I had of the men taunting Rose and myself before I tipped us over the edge to our deaths. I was never the threat. Their fear was. It was the fear of what they did not understand that consumed them. Their quickness to latch onto the herd mentality instead of questioning whether what was seen as right might have actually been wrong.

My chest began to heave as anger coursed through me, until suddenly it clicked. Their faces. I had seen them again....

Fury flowed through my body, and I could feel the warm topple down my cheeks as it escaped me through my tear ducts.

Clenching my fists, I looked around frantically, as if I hoped someone would take away this new piercing pain that shot through my body as this new hell descended over me.

My Higher Self must have been eavesdropping in my brain because she stepped forward and said to me, "You can no longer align with that energy, Annalyse. You must only observe the information. By aligning with something, you create more of the same energy. By observing it and seeing what needs to be healed and transcended, you are able to do just that."

I scowled at her with my fists clenched at my sides.

"THIS IS WHAT YOU SAY TO ME AFTER WHAT I JUST REALIZED!?" I screamed within the chamber, and my voice echoed around in perfect synchronization with the pain I had just retrieved from the revelation I just had.

"THOSE SAME MEN WHO CAUSED ROSE'S AND MY DEATHS WERE THE SAME TO MURDER ME AGAIN!?"

After this new declaration of torment rung through the cavern, there was only silence.

And it was deafening.

I dropped to my knees and cried.

It was ironic to me to think that they were all so worried about how difficult it would be for me to go through the Barnium Portal to retrieve the origination of the Mirror Souls memory, but it was this memory that was excruciating to process. In two separate lifetimes, these men were responsible for taking my life and separating me from Michael.

I was not aware of how long I cried, and, since time worked differently here, there was really no way to quantify it.

My heart ached. Why was the world so cruel?

My Higher Self came to stand in front of me then lowered herself to her knees before sitting on her heels. Lifting my chin she said, "Souls do not want to hurt other souls. It is at great cost to them. It is through the disconnection from their true self, creation, and love that this began to happen. The result has been devastating, as this karma is very difficult to rebalance. Taking another's life causes the soul who performed the act to be indebted to the soul they took, it also causes the soul who was removed prematurely from the physical plane to have to reincarnate and start over. It is impossible to explain the chaos that this can cause."

"How could these men's souls have possibly been in debt to me if they committed such an atrocious act against me?"

My Higher Self's answer was the last thing I expected.

"Because, during your pre-incarnation session, they agreed to. They made a soul contract."

"*What?*" I exclaimed. "Why would they have agreed to do that?"

"Because they were indebted to you."

I stared at her blankly. That was clearly and understatement but how could their indebtedness lead them to kill me? Again.

"Like I said," she continued. "It is a very heavy price to pay for a soul who has willingly, with desire and pleasure, taken a life. It traumatizes the soul far more than the physical body who exited the physical plane. Souls who do this must incarnate into situations that are a living hell, for many lifetimes, in order to balance their karma. In this lifetime, you had to die in order to come back into your true body and the act had to be traumatic enough to trigger your Awakening. Those men's souls agreed to be the ones to do it for you as an act of penance for their original sin against you, knowing it was something that you needed to happen in order to fulfill your destiny. I assure you, it was a great sacrifice those souls made, and it was in service to you."

Dear god....

Thinking about those men brought my thoughts back to Henry.

I looked frantically at my Higher Self and asked, "But Henry! He's ok right?"

I turned to find Galstar in the crowd that was standing around me.

"You said what I was feeling was me trying to pull his soul to cross over, which meant he had to still be in the physical realm. Please tell me he is still alive and okay!"

Galstar stepped forward out of the crowd and said, "Henry is a bit sore, but he is physically whole."

Oh thank god.

"Is Henry aware of what is happening? Of our communication right now?"

"Yes and no. He is very worried about you, but he is learning what he must along his own journey as well. Because of your deep pain a few moments ago, the sorrow passed on to your physical body causing it to also shed tears. This change in your physical state triggered your previous nurse Annie to let him know there was a change with you. He had asked her to keep him informed of your condition when your body first arrived at the hospital, due to his guilt as a result of the accident. He is now with your physical body and can feel you close to him. There are shifts and changes going on inside him that he is not currently aware of. The awakening is a slow process, but Henry was already primed and ready for his activation. He will assimilate the information relatively easily and begin to remember who he truly is and the knowledge that comes with it. Just like you, he needs an IV drip, not the whole bag at once."

"He must be worried sick," I said. My heart ached thinking about what he must be going through.

"Yes, he is. But that is part of his journey. The masculine has struggled under the weight of control and the need to fix things in an attempt to assert and gain that control. This is part of his transformation and healing. He cannot fix you because you are not broken and do not need to be fixed. The need for control must be surrendered. That is the only way he will find you."

"Can't I go back now? Now that this so called activation is completed?" I asked looking back and forth between my and Henry's Over Souls.

It was mine who answered.

"I'm afraid your journey here is not complete. You, yourself have more healing to do and a choice that you must make before you can rejoin Henry in the physical."

"I thought I had already made the choice. When I was in the Transitory Plane, I told Galstar that I chose to go back."

"You cannot," Galstar said.

"What? Why? I don't understand." I was almost on the verge of tears again.

"You are not allowing yourself to move forward," my Higher Self explained.

"Wait. You're telling me that I am the one keeping myself here now?"

"Yes, Annalyse," she replied with a hint of sympathy.

"Well, how do I get out? What do I need to do?"

"You have a choice to make," she repeated again.

"What do I need to do?" I reiterated, looking around at the crowd of guides standing around me. "Just tell me and I will do it. I want to get back! I want to get back to Henry!"

"If that were true, you would have already left when Ky reawakened in the Divine Masculine form. Right now, Annalyse, you're looking for a way out when you need to be going in."

I looked at Ky with confusion and then back at my Higher Self. This made no sense.

"How do I get back to Henry?" I asked flatly.

I was tired of the riddles and confusion and just wanted to return to Henry. I could imagine how much he was worrying about me and it made my

102

heart ache to think about the level of pain he must be going through. All I wanted was to be able to place my hand on the side of his face, gaze into his beautiful blue eyes, and tell him 'I'm back."

"We can take you where you need to go, but from there it is all up to you. We cannot tell you what to do. It must be a free will choice," my Higher Self told me.

"What must be?"

"You will know, when you are ready."

I took a deep breath of surrender, tilted my head back, and rolled my eyes.

"Of course I will. Fine, take me where I need to go."

I had absolutely no idea where I was being sent or what I needed to do, but it did not matter. All I knew was there was nothing more that I wanted than to be reunited with Henry.

Or so I thought.

Ky and my Higher Self looked at each other for a moment before Ky gestured over to what appeared to be a large slab of quartz. It looked like it was carved to be an altar or medical table for operating, and it was nearby the glass cases filled with healing implements.

"Regulus and Sirius will assist you," my Higher Self told me, as she gestured for me to lay down on the quartz alter.

Two regal looking white lions, who stood upright like humans, made their way over to me as I laid back on the hard stone. This felt familiar to me, as if I had been here before, but in a dream. I suddenly had flashes of memories coming back of me laying on this table as a team of sentient and celestial beings used other-worldly instruments to do healing work on me.

I looked over at Ky and my Higher Self one last time. "Wait," I said, looking at my Higher Self. "If he," I flicked my chin in Ky's direction, "has a name. Then what is yours?"

She smiled and said, "It's Theia."

"Theia," I said as I smiled at her before turning my face back towards the ceiling and closing my eyes.

When I regained consciousness, I knew immediately that I was not in my own bed. The mattress felt strange and uneven, like someone had stuffed it with random things in hopes of making something suitable for sleeping. Before opening my eyes, I tried to get a feel for the space as best I could from my other senses since I did not know what type of environment or situation I was walking into. I could smell soot or burned wood, as if from a wood fire that had burned itself out. I moved my body around a bit, to try to get a feel for it, making sure everything was functioning properly. I first started by slowly wiggling my toes and fingers, feeling that they were bare against the bedding I was laying in. I felt as if I were wearing a long night gown and no under garments.

Slowly I edged my arms away from my body, spreading them out. What I discovered made my eyes snap open.

There was something next to me and by the feel of the hand that mine brushed up against under the covers, it was definitely a person.

Hopeful I was back with Henry, my eyes popped open and I looked around, only to realize I was not in his bed, much less his bedroom.

I was not even in his timeline.

I was lying in a four-poster bed with a red canopy, in what I could only describe as an "old" bedroom. As I gazed around, attempting to not move much, I noticed there was nothing modern about the space. There were no electronics, no photographs, and no noise. It was eerily quiet. There was absolutely no noise besides that coming from right next to me – the deep, methodical breaths of someone in a deep sleep.

I slowly turned my head to look at where the sound was coming from and when my eyes made contact with the source of the sound, I felt ice spread through my veins.

Lying in bed next to me was a sleeping man. His hair was dark and slightly disheveled from the previous night's sleep and he had a strong jaw line, peppered with dark stubble.

I knew immediately who this man was. I would have recognized him anywhere.

His name slipped from my lips in a disbelieving whisper.

"Michael...?"

CHAPTER 6
Henry

Everything was dark and damp.

I could feel the hum of the planet as it cradled me like it was a transformative cocoon. I couldn't see anything, but I could feel everything. I could feel the whole earth taking long, slow breaths, I could feel the soothing and comforting energy gently rocking me as if I were a baby being carried in a safe and comforting womb.

I was of the Earth and I was in the Earth.

I was the Earth.

Was I dead?

I kenned immediately after asking the question that the answer was "no."

I was not dead.

*I was quite the opposite. I was one with the Earth.
The great mother of creation that supported every
breath I take as one of her inhabitants. We were
one. Connected. I needed her to survive and she
needed me too. We were in a partnership of
cocreation and I was beginning to come alive. It
was as if I had been balled up like a seed and
planted into the ground. I thought to try to stretch
out and see just how far I could grow and I was
pleased and surprised to learn that my growth was
without limit. The ground moved with me, as if
eager to show my limbs the way. Wanting me to
move through her and transform into what I was
being called to be.*

What she was calling me to be.

*The further I stretched, the further I grew until I felt
my entire body rise up out of the ground like a
volcano rising from the core of the Earth. I was
huge. Like the tallest mountain. I looked out across
the Earth eager to see her wonderment but instead
I was met with quite the opposite.*

*I found myself in utter shock and disbelief. As I
surveyed the land, it was as if it had been
destroyed. Raped, pillaged, plundered, exploited.
Torn to bits as all of her viability had been snatched
up and stolen from her, with no regard to her and
what gifts she offers to mankind. I felt shame and*

disgust as I took witness to the repercussions of her violent objectification.

The oceans were filled with trash and smelled of putrid death, the forests were cut, mangled, and dead, animals laid waste on the ground, slaughtered by the millions, and there were hot spots all along the surface of the planet where hot lava was pouring up out of the earth. Watching the core of my mother pour out along her surface made my heart ache. It was as if she was bleeding.

She was bleeding all over herself.

As I looked around at the utter destruction, the sudden realization struck me that I was the one responsible for this. It had been my lust and desire to control, consume, own, and conquer that nearly killed my own mother. My one and only true source of sustenance and key to my survival. The home of the Divine Feminine energy. The home of love, of nurturing, and of creation. Through my blindness, I almost destroyed my home and the power in it to create. I almost destroyed myself, for we were connected, she and I. We were one. We are one. One could not do something without having an effect on the other.

The heartache grew as I began to hear whispers from the trees, the animals, and the oceans. They *were crying out to me. Pleading. Begging me to hear their call.*

"Wake up, wake up, wake up," they kept saying, and I began to weep.

As I wept for the loss of my beloved, I was utterly shocked to witness that where my tears landed on the ground I could see the earth turning green. It was as if by giving her my love, I began to restore Her, so I surrendered to the pain and no longer tried to deny my part in it or act like it did not exist. I accepted what was and the role I played in the atrocities that destroyed Her. There was no condemnation of accusation. It was not needed. I could see before me the truth, so I simply allowed myself to grieve for Her and I opened my heart to Her.

"Wake up, wake up, wake up..."

It was in this moment that I felt my eyes were truly open for the first time in the history of my physical existences. I saw the truth that we were not enemies. We were one living being, living together with varying consciousnesses. I realized how foolish I had been in my thinking to assume that just because I had a unique perspective of our collective experience that somehow that equaled my being separate from it.

"Wake up, wake up, wake up..."

As my tears continued to splash upon her surface, I could feel her responding to me.

Responding to my love.

"Aye, dear lass. Forgive me," I said, as I felt Her connecting with me as her energy reached out for me. I could feel her forgiveness. I could feel her love. It filled every cell in my body as I was consumed with radiant, white light. I allowed my love for Her to flow through me and back into Her as we healed each other.

It was in this moment, that I felt whole.

As I shared in the intimacy with the Divine Feminine, I continued to hear the whispers.

"Wake up, wake up, wake up..."

The deeper I connected with Her, the louder and louder the whispers grew.

"Wake up, wake up, wake up..."

Until....

"Henry, wake up."

"Huh, what?" I said, as I looked around in confusion.

There was a middle-aged, red-haired woman standing in front of me with her face inches from mine, studying me.

"Shannon?" I said as I tried to wipe the sleep from my eyes. "Shannon, is that you?"

As I pulled my hands away from my face, I noticed they had some tears on them. I quickly wiped my cheeks to remove any more remnants of my emotions that had escaped while I had been asleep.

I rubbed the back of my neck, to try to relieve some of the tension from its stiff muscles that rebelled against my uncomfortable sleeping arrangements, as I stood up to shake Shannon's hand.

"Shannon, I am so grateful to have you here. It means so much that you would make this trip to assist us," I told her as our hands shook.

She watched me intently, as if she was not sure what she saw or what she was looking for.

"What is it?" I asked her.

"It's your aura," she said as she continued to look at me with a furrowed brow, while she cocked her head from side to side.

"What about it?" I asked, as I watched her watching me.

"It's shifting. It's always been an aqua-teal color, but now I see other colors in it."

"I do not ken what that means. Is this something to be of concern about?" I asked her.

"No. Not necessarily. And what is bad anyway? It's usually just something that represents an experience not bending to our will. It's just something to observe, is all. What I am more interested in knowing is where you were."

Her lips pursed as she looked at me.

I did not have a clue what she was referring to.

In all truth, I really liked Shannon, but being around her made me uncomfortable. It was as if she was on a whole other level and could hear and see things that were past my comprehension. I constantly felt out of the loop when I was around her, as if she and other worldly beings were having silent conversations that I was not privy to.

"I do not ken what you are referring to," I said honestly. "I have not gone anywhere since you and I last spoke on the phone. I have been here with Annalyse, resting."

"When you were resting you had a dream, did you not?

"Aye, I did. How is that relevant to Annalyse?" I asked, beginning to feel self-conscious that my face might be betraying me with tear stains.

"That wasn't just a dream Henry. You went somewhere." Taking a step closer to me she asked in a low tone, "What did they show you?"

The words she used stuck out to me. "What did *they* show you?"

"What did *who* show me?" I pressed.

"Your guides. I know you were in the astral plane just before I came in. I could feel your energy and that of many other beings. Including her," she said as she gestured past me to Annalyse.

"You could feel her here? With me?"

"No. I could feel you there with her. Then your energies parted and you each went somewhere else. Can't you feel it? Do you still feel your connection to her?"

I hadn't even noticed until she brought my attention to it, but the butterflies were gone and in there space was again the gaping black hole that had existed in my chest most of my life.

I immediately went to Annalyse's side expecting to see that she had actually died, but her heart monitor still beeped just as it had done before.

Breathing suddenly became very difficult, so I sat back down in the chair next to Annalyse's bed. I then looked up at Shannon in despair.

"Where did she go?" I asked. The agony was prevalent in my voice. As much as I fought to stay strong, for Annalyse, for us, the pain was undisguisable, and my voice betrayed me. "Did she find a new body? Do you think she will be able to find me? What does this mean?! I do not ken what I am supposed to do now! Where did she go?"

As I spoke, I held Annalyse's hand up to my face and began sobbing into the back of it. I could feel her soft skin reflecting back the warmth of my breath as it struck at her with every sob.

I kenned Shannon watched me as I agonized. I could feel her eyes on me and kenned that she had compassion for me and was holding back her answers because she kenned I would not like them. Or perhaps she didn't quite ken how to tell me.

"Please, Shannon," I pleaded as I pulled my face away from Annalyse's hand and looked up at her from the chair. "Please tell me what I need to do."

It was clear to me that she was considering all options and trying to guide me as best she could, yet her response surprised me.

"Would you like to introduce me to your Mirror Soul?" she said as she walked around Annalyse's bed to stand on the opposite side of it from me.

"My what?" I said as I stared at her with confusion. I had never heard that term, yet found it interesting that she used it, as I called Annalyse my Anam Faileas. In essence, it means that I see her as my own soul's reflection.

Shannon was staring at Annalyse as I asked my question and continued to stare at her when she answered.

"It appears someone has been keeping secrets."

"What do you mean?" I asked.

Lifting her gaze to meet mine, Shannon answered, "I guess I have some explaining to do."

She sat down in the chair across from me and looked me square in the eyes.

"You must be in agony," she said, very matter of fact.

"Aye," I responded with a nod. "I feel like I am dying."

"Henry," she said as she leaned forward slightly, "I'm afraid that's because you are."

This was not at all what I had expected her to say. I sat back in my chair in shock.

"What? How? Why would I be dying?"

"Your souls are linked." She paused for a moment to allow this information to sink in, but I did not need the pause. I had already kenned that Annalyse had been Sara during the lifetime that I was Michael and that we were soulmates.

I nodded in encouragement for her to continue.

"It's not as you think it is Henry. You two are more than past life lovers or even soulmates. You are *unum et anima una***.**"

"I do not ken what that means," I told her as my brow furrowed.

"It means you are one soul. The same soul that incarnated into both the male and female expression in order to mirror itself. Your soul, the one assigned to you and Annalyse, is the original soul stream that began the human race."

After she finished this statement, all I could hear was the pounding of blood in my ears.

How could what she said possibly be true?

Could it be possible? I pondered for a moment and thought about what Shannon just said. It made sense that the human race had to start somewhere with someone. Why not me?

I shook my head a little bit, hoping that would help settle all the thoughts that were now floating through my head like pieces of snow in a snow globe that has just been shaken.

"How do you ken this, Shannon?" I asked.

"Because I had a dream about it last night," she said matter-of-factly.

"Truly? Tell me what you saw. What happened in the dream?"

"I watched as a being from another time and race was struck by lightning, while the planet was almost destroyed. The lighting split it into two parts. The masculine and the feminine. That being was you," she explained and then looked down at Annalyse, "and her. I then saw a conference of guides and ethereal beings meeting to explain to Annalyse what happened and all that I am filling you in on. You need to know, just as she needed to know."

"I'm still not understanding why that would mean that I am dying," I said.

"It's because your soul is the same, Henry. In order for you to continue to exist here in the physical, your soul must be here with you."

"But we have been apart before. And as much as it felt like I was dying all that time, I never did."

"Yes, Henry. But her soul was here, in this plane and this dimension. So, as much as you felt like you were in separation, that was simply an illusion. In this case, it is different. Her soul is in a different realm. If her soul remains there, yours will eventually separate and have to follow."

"I don't care. I would follow her anywhere to be with her."

"I understand that, Henry, but it cannot happen this way. There is so much more at stake than you realize."

"Then tell me," I said, beginning to feel frustrated.

I kenned it made me seem like a petulant child, but it stung to hear that these "guides" were talking to Annalyse and even Shannon, but not to *me*. I deserved answers too.

"You two have a purpose here. Humanity has been sleeping for millennia as the collective soul has been healing from the trauma of the soul split. It is time for them to awaken and to heal. Your soul was the one who started everything and now it is time to wake up humanity. If you do not, you saw what will continue to happen, did you not?"

The flashes of the dream I had been having before Shannon woke me up flickered through my mind and I shuddered.

"After the collective soul split, there was much trauma and with that came a lot of pain and suffering. The two of you only incarnated in mirror form three times during the last few thousands of years as the collective soul has worked to mend itself. Once as Adam and Lilith as the original split, though the patriarchy later portrayed Lilith as Eve in order to further suppress and condemn the feminine. The second time you incarnated as Michael and Sara, and then again in this lifetime as Annalyse and Henry. The mirror soul incarnation is a very challenging one. The best way to heal one's soul is to take a deep, hard look at oneself.

One of the most difficult parts of the healing journey is when we have to take responsibility for how fucked up our lives are and realize that no matter what was done to us, at this point it is up to us to deal with the consequences. We do this by either letting the actions of others or circumstances out of our control destroy us, or by deciding that the suffering stops here and now, and that it is time to change the story by changing how we speak about it, and begin writing a new one, consciously.

When you incarnate as mirrors, you are forced to look deeply inside at your true woundings, in order to be forced to heal them. As you heal them, you heal them for the collective soul. This is why you came here like this. It was not to find your true love. It was to embody true love by being it. Together."

Shannon paused for a moment, looked closely at Annalyse, and then continued with a brief shake of her head.

"Unfortunately, it has been the feminine energy that has been on the receiving end of the pain. As you can see." She gestured at the state of Annalyse, referring to what had happened the night before to force her back into her own body. "But that is because she is the stronger and more powerful energy, having the ability to heal the woundings and the collective wound by creating new, with her womb.

Humanity has been raging against the feminine energy for eons, and the strongest source of this energy is our own Mother Earth. If humanity continues down the road that it is on, it will completely consume and destroy her.

You must wake them up. It is your destiny. If you do not wake them, we will have to start all over again like we did before with the original soul split. No one would remember, but you. Knowing how much suffering was involved in order to get here, could you condemn us all to having to go through all of it again?"

As I listened to Shannon speak, I almost felt as if I were a spectator in the conversation as a third party. If someone had said something like this to me even a week ago, I would have thought them to be mad. But as she spoke, it was almost as if I were remembering everything as she said it.

"Henry," Shannon continued, and in an effort to bring my attention back to her I looked her in the eyes before she added, "you must bring her back. Humanity depends on it."

"I want to," I said. "I do not ken how to get to her or where she is. I thought I could use our soul connection to help me find her in the astral plane, but now that it's gone I do not ken what to do. Where did she go?"

I could tell that is next part of this information dump that Shannon was giving me was a particularly difficult message to deliver by the change in her energy and tone.

"Henry, she went home."

"So, you mean she crossed over? How could I retrieve her from the other side? And how is her body still functioning?"

"No, Henry," she responded. "She has not crossed over. That is why her body is still alive."

"Then I do not understand. I do not get why earlier I could feel her, and now I cannot. How and why would that change if she has not gone anywhere else?"

Shannon took a deep breath before leveling her blow.

"You cannot feel her soul anymore, because she has given it away to someone else."

The words hit me like a prize fight strike. If I had not already been sitting down, they would have knocked me clean off my feet.

"She what?" I said in a whisper as my already broken heart began to splinter. "How could she…?"

My words trailed off as the pain threated to choke me.

I could not wrap my head around how this could happen or what this meant, until it clicked.

I snapped my head up to look at Shannon and asked in a whisper, *"The devil?"*

"No, Henry." Her tone was almost chastising, as if it was a silly thing I had just suggested.

"Then who could possibly have taken her soul?" I asked.

"No one took it. She gave it willingly."

I could not understand. How and who could she possibly want to be with more than me? Her Mirror Soul.

"Who Shannon? Who did she give her soul to?"

She took another deep breath and then said, "You."

"What? Why must you torment me with these riddles!?" I shouted louder than I meant to. "That does not make any sense. If she gave her soul to me, would she not be back here with me?"

Shannon watched me closely as if to gauge if I could handle the answer. Whatever she saw must have told her that I could, though she was wrong.

"She didn't give it to this version of you, Henry. She gave it to Michael."

CHAPTER 7

Michael opened his eyes sleepily, and I inhaled sharply.

What if he did not know who I was? What if he did not remember me, and he woke to see some random woman in his bed.

Would he shout out or attack me?

I lay frozen, unsure of what I should or should not do.

The sound of my intake of breath must have called to his attention because he turned his head in my direction, and when he laid his eyes on me he gave me a sheepish half smile.

I had never in my life seen something so magnificent, and immediately every muscle in my body relaxed.

I was safe.

Safer than I had ever been in my life.

I was with Michael.

"Good morning, my queen," he said as he looked at me through sleep heavy lids.

After hearing him speak, there was a part of me that thought for a moment how strange it was that his dialog and accent sounded so similar to mine and didn't have the old Scottish lilt to it, but I dismissed the thought quickly, assuming it was simply because the way he spoke just seemed normal to me like any person who is used to their home dialect and accent wouldn't hear anything strange or different.

I rolled completely onto my side so that I was face to face with him.

Michael.

Here he was.

The man who had held my heart for over thirty years, though we had actually never met, was lying with his face inches from mine. I simply laid there and stared at him, taking in his features in awe. I could tell that he was watching me, but I didn't mind. I felt completely comfortable here with him. I had known this man my whole life and he probably knew me better than any person I had physically interacted with during my life span.

My eyes jumped around his face, taking in every feature of him. It was if they danced around in ecstasy as they fed on him being in front of them instead of behind them, only seen in the imagery of my third eye. There had never been a more satisfying sight to behold but the perfection directly before me. If my eyes could have known thirst, Michael's face would have been the perfect quenching tonic they craved.

My eyes moved from his lovely blue ones, to every inch of his face. He had a mild notch in his strong chin that finalized his strong jawline and one dark eyebrow was slightly higher than the other.

Huh… I thought to myself. *His face isn't perfectly symmetrical either, yet, in its own right, it is utterly and completely perfect.* It was odd to find an "imperfection" in his features when I had always seen him as the epitome of perfection.

I still did. Nothing would ever change that.

Seeing him before me, I was completely enraptured by him. It was as if he was the one who could do magic, and I was helpless against his powerful spell. I could no longer tolerate my eyes being the only sense that experienced him so I brought my hand up to touch the stubble on his cheek, and, with that one caress, I could feel a deluge of emotions wash though me as the familiarity of how it felt to touch him registered in every inch of my body.

Tears welled up in my eyes, and I could feel their warmth as they slowly slid sideways down my face.

Michael's brow furrowed in response to my tears and I hungerly placed my fingers in the lines between his eyebrows. I wanted to touch every emotion he experienced. I wanted to feel how it felt to him.

He must have wanted something different from me because he reached up, grabbed my hand, and moved it away from his face to look at me. The contact felt like an invisible form of liquid light, made purely out of dopamine, had been placed on my skin where his hand connected with mine and it spread through my body like a warm breeze.

"What is it, lass?" he asked me while concern was evident on his face. "Was it another bad dream? They cannot hurt you anymore. I am here now. You're safe."

A bad dream?

That must have been what had happened. I must have had a very vivid, bad dream. I always hated when that happened. When everything in the dream felt so real that, even after you woke, it took a few moments to decipher what was real and what had merely been occurring in your mind.

"Yes," I said. "It must have been," I added more in an effort to convince myself.

It was the only plausible answer.

Michael looked at me with kindness and compassion as he gently stroked the side of my face, brushing some of my hair off my cheek. I closed my eyes and allowed the pleasurable sensation of his fingertips sliding across my skin, as they left their traces of the liquid light, to have my full attention.

"Tell me, my darling," Michael said. "Tell me what you dreamed about that upset you so."

Keeping my eyes closed so that I could pull up the memories more clearly, I told him all about being a child and remembering him but never understanding who he was or how I could have even known him, but the loss of him ached inside me nevertheless. I told him about growing up feeling a gaping whole in my chest that made taking a full breath difficult. I told him about dating other men and how they never seemed to satisfy me on a deep spiritual and emotional level because I knew they weren't him.

I even told him about a man named Henry that I had met and how I thought I had found him again but then was torn away from him, as I was brutally assaulted, only to end up in a white room surrounded by all types of beings who showed me visons of being torn in two and being attacked and consumed by my other half. I told him about Theia and how she told me I had a choice to make and that I could not go straight home until I made it and how she had me lay down on a large clear-white stone table as I was put to sleep by two lion-men.

As I recounted my dream for Michael his hand traveled from my face to my own hand and held it in support as I shared with him everything I had experienced.

"And when I woke up, I was here," I said as I had come to the end of my story. "I'm so glad I woke up next to you," I added as I finally opened my eyes.

Michael gave me a large smile in response.

"Me too. Though I am sorry that you had to experience all those terrible things. You are here now, with me and you are completely safe. This Theia creature was obviously wrong because you did come home. You came to where you truly wanted to be. Where you belong and where nothing can hurt you here while you are with me. Just stay close, and I will take care of you."

How could I possibly argue with that?

I nodded in response to his instructions.

Leaning forward he placed a kiss on my lips.

His lips felt so good against mine. They were full and soft. The contact set a firework off inside my stomach, just behind my belly button. It was as if the sensation placed a cord between the two of us, forcing the need for my body to be placed right up against his own.

There was a faint whisper of a voice in the back of my mind that tried to tell me how strange this situation was – how I had literally woken up next to a man who I completely believed I had never met, and now I was ready to completely hand myself over to him. But I dismissed it quickly.

Michael had said it was all a dream, and that made so much sense to me now, in this moment, as nothing else had ever felt so real than this moment, right now, lying next to Michael. I wanted this more than anything. I always had, and I would shut down any limiting thought that might pop up that would try to steal it away from me.

I slightly shimmied my body towards him, closing the small gap between us. It just felt so right to be close to him. There was no fear or anxiety. Just a need for physical connection that I wanted to satisfy. I could feel my breasts pressing against his strong, broad chest, and, as I rocked my hips forward to push them into him, I could feel his desire was strong for me, as well, in response. He and I were not the only things that had just woken up this morning.

Michael was a large man and I could feel that proportions were favorable to his physical size. My body responded to the feeling of his desire with a rush of blood that would prepare me to receive him. I longed to connect with him in this way, and my body was fully in alignment with this physical desire. I could feel the buzz of the hormones charging through my bloodstream as my heartrate began to pick up and my breathing hastened.

Recognizing the shift in my body was all the invitation Michael needed to fulfill my desire and meet my need. He was more than eager to give me what my eyes and body were both screaming out for.

Him.

Taking the arm that he had been laying on, he gently slid it under my neck, then bent his hand down to hold the back of my head as we placed our foreheads against one another's. I could tell he was using his other hand to free himself of his pants before dragging it slowly up my leg, lifting the skirt of my night gown up past my hips. He then took my thigh and pulled my leg up over his before placing his upper leg between my own. The whole time he prepared our bodies for union, he simply held my head and peered deeply into my eyes.

The level of intimacy was unmatched by anything I had ever experienced. Watching me closely he slowly glided over my skin as his hand made its way past my thigh towards my more sensitive area. His eyes closed as he redirected that sense to his sense of touch, and he let out a contented sigh accompanied by a small smile when he felt the confirmation of my arousal. My hips rolled in anticipation, hearing his sigh of pleasure at my body's physical response of wanting him. Michael's eyes snapped open as he quickly lined himself up with me, then placed his hand on my hip to pull me onto him.

As he entered me, my eyes closed, and the grip he had on the roots of my hair tightened. I opened my eyes again to stare into the depth of his, as he slowly rocked his hips back and forth while inside me. His free hand made its way to my breasts and then to my shoulder where he utilized the grip for leverage.

We laid there, side by side as the intoxicating bliss spread through my body while we connected. There was an energetic loop between us that started in the physical and maintained its link energetically through our deep eye connection. I felt like I could see my own soul as I gazed into Michael's eyes. It was intoxicating. The level of power created from being able to tap into one's self on such a deep level was a type of high that many would dream of, but few would ever be able to achieve.

I felt like I was literally making love, creating it in massive abundant flow, with my own soul. I was tapping into the ability to energetically mate with the entire universe.

This was Nirvana.

And I never wanted it to end.

The world could have come crashing down around us, and I would not have cared.

I wanted this.

I had wanted it for as long as I could remember. It felt right. It felt familiar.

He felt right. He felt familiar. He felt like mine.

And I felt like I was the luckiest woman in the world to have all of it.

I felt so foolish for having had given so much credence to my bad dream. It had felt so real that I had not been able to decipher truth from fantasy. I guess that's the thing with our mind. It is all real to us. If we can think it, we imagine it, and our body responds as if it is really happening. How can we ever truly know what is real or not when we can create in such a way?

The truth was, I could not possibly care less at this point.

"Reality" or not, this *was* my reality right now, in this moment, and I felt like I had wanted it forever.

So, I gave in.

I was tired of suffering. I was tired of the struggle. It felt so good to feel so good. To feel safe and to be able to ultimately surrender into my physical wants and desires without them being clouded by overthinking, fear, insecurity, or pain from past experiences, was a whole level of bliss that I had never known I was capable of experiencing. This was pure, unbridled, intimacy and instead of ruining it with my own thoughts, I submitted to it. To him.

And it felt so fucking good.

He rolled me up on top of him and then whispered, "Give me your mouth."

I was happy to oblige.

My lips parted in invitation for him to connect with me. Reaching his hands up under my arms he slid them onto my upper back and curled his fingers around my shoulders to hold them. He used this grip to create leverage as he increased in force and speed underneath me.

I moaned into his mouth, as be pounded against me.

This all felt so natural.

The ability to surrender to the pleasure of the sexual connection Michael and I had was as easy as breathing.

He pulled my face back from his slightly so that our eyes could connect. As the energy built between our bodies and souls, I could feel a warmth growing inside my chest until finally it released through my body like some type of energetic firework that exploded within me and consuming every inch of my body with ecstatic bliss.

My head arched back as I closed my eyes, allowing the energy to surge through me in complete surrender. Though I had never experienced it before or known what it was called, I knew in that moment that I had experienced what I could only describe as a "soul-gasm." It was as if the energetic being that resided in my physical body experienced its own version of an orgasm.

Michael reduced his motions as he allowed me to regain myself and my composure. I looked down at him to see a broad smile on his face.

"Ah, my love," he said as he slowly moved his hands down my arms as I sat up astride him. "I felt you inside me too."

I knew he was referring to our soul connection and how he felt my own respond to him.

I smiled back in reply.

Taking advantage my of new mounted position, I took the responsibility of determining our rhythm. I allowed my body to take over and arched my back as my hips rolled against his.

"That's it, my darling. Let go," he whispered as his hands slid across my breasts, rolling my nipples between his thumb and index finger.

Wanting to feel more of his skin on mine, I pulled my night dress off over my head to expose every inch of myself to him. I then leaned forward to place my breast in his mouth. The extra stimulation pushed me over the edge as I climaxed around him. Feeling my release, he gave into his own.

I could feel him relax under my body, as the pleasure surged through his own.

The joy I felt knowing I brought this beautiful man so much pleasure painted a fresh smile on my face.

My heart pounded as I leaned forward to lay down on his chest while still astride him. Even after developing a sheen of sweat on his skin, he still smelled amazing.

Like home.

He gently stroked my hair as I listed to his heart rate slow to a normal resting rhythm. I loved the way his chest hair felt against the skin on my cheek.

I lifted myself up a bit to look at his face.

"You are my heaven," he said as he brought one of my hands up to his mouth and placed a kiss at the base of my palm before placing it on the side of his face.

The truth was, he was my heaven too.

He was the most beautiful thing I had ever seen, and as I stared at him, I could not understand why I ever felt any sort of separation or disconnection from him, as he had obviously been here the entire time.

Regardless of this fact, I looked him in the eyes, while my hand still rested on the side of his face and said, "I'm back, and I am never leaving your side."

CHAPTER 8
Henry

I had to go home.

I felt guilty leaving Annalyse, but I could not possibly stay in the hospital any longer. Thanks to my overpowering exhaustion every nerve in my body felt exposed, and my senses felt like they had been turned up several notches. I could not stand the sterile smell, the grey walls and floors. It made me feel as if I were in a prison.

I already felt trapped as it was. I did not need the walls of the hospital closing in on me making me feel more claustrophobic. The building had begun to feel more like an insane asylum than a place of healing and I could not handle it anymore.

Shannon had urged me to leave and to go home to get some rest and to freshen up. I only agreed because she had promised to stay with Annalyse until Morgan or I had returned. I appreciated her commitment to Annalyse and the journey she was on.

I kenned that she was right, of course. I was of no good to Annalyse in my condition. I was dirty, worn out, terrified, frustrated, and completely overwhelmed. If I was to be able to find answers and be open to solutions, I needed a clear head that was rested and open to receiving, and I needed my body to be refreshed and strong in order to support my spirit and its connection with Annalyse.

By the time I got home I had not even realized that I was there. The thought horrified me that I had been so out of it, I had no recollection of my drive home and that I had been in such a state of autopilot while driving. How dangerous, yet also reaffirming to the fact that I needed some true rest. The thought of what could have happened on my drive home made me shudder. I had already been responsible for one deadly car crash, I did not think my soul could possibly handle the weight of another.

After making my way slowly into the house, I went into the kitchen to get a glass of water. I stood in my kitchen in front of the sink as the water from the faucet filled my glass. In standard cases, I would never dream of drinking water from a faucet with all the chemicals in regular tap water, but, since I had a well and a state of the art filtration system, I loved the water I got straight from the tap. It was so pure and refreshing, it may as well have been from a fresh spring being directed straight into my house.

As the water filled the glass, I stared out the window in front of me and out towards the tree line where the woods began at the edge of the grassy field. I thought of all the life that lived in those woods, and the dream I had experienced while waiting for Shannon's arrival. I envisioned that forest dead and broken as I had seen it in my vision and wondered how much death I would have been responsible for if I had been the reason behind that chaos. It was a dark thought that matched my dark mood.

Without warning, the water began to overflow from the glass, snapping me out of my macabre daydream. The cool dampness of the water touched my skin, forcing me to return to the present.

I took advantage of the unintended wetness on my hand and rubbed it on the back of my neck, in the hopes that it would soothe the fire that was raging several inches higher inside my head.

My brain was on overload.

I was grateful to Shannon and her role in being able to tap into the information on the other side of the veil for me, but still, I wished none of it were true. How could I have chosen this path? How could Annalyse? Why could we not just simply enjoy each other and live happily ever after?

Why did it feel like my life was always filled with sacrifice?

God, I was so tired.

Physically, mentally, and emotionally, then adding the guilt that came along with feeling responsible for what was happening with Annalyse *and* leaving her in that cold, sterile, stone box while I came home?

I felt like I was the most worthless piece of shit in existence.

I hated leaving Annalyse there at the hospital, but Shannon was right. I had to get some separation, especially after what she told me about Michael. It was very difficult for me to process what I had learned about why Annalyse wasn't waking up. I felt so betrayed. Here I was, in absolute torment and agony over what happened to her, and instead of coming back to me to work through things with me, she chose to mentally go back in time to be with a past life version of myself?

She had given her soul to Michael?

I could not begin to understand this.

Michael and I were the same. Just different physical expressions in different timelines. Why would she rather be with him than with me? The pain of that level of dismissal was extraordinary. Never had I felt such deep betrayal and rejection. It was emotionally excruciating, and, to make it worse, I was literally jealous of myself, but myself from a different lifetime. How could I possibly make sense of that?

My head was spinning as I downed my water in one large gulp, then placed the glass on the counter. I did not see the point in putting it away, as I kenned I would be coming back for more shortly.

Exhaustion was fighting to overtake me, but I needed to shower before I could lay myself down in bed. Just as I was making my way to the bedroom, Jordan came in through the garage entrance.

"Mornin'," he said. "I saw yer car in the garage, so I wanted to check in on ye."

That's when it hit me that Jordan only kenned Annalyse as Vivien and that Vivien was now dead, according to the information presented when I had texted him and told him what happened. He had no idea that Annalyse was now lost in some cosmic space reality with a past life version of myself or who Annalyse even was.

How in God's name would I even begin to try to explain something like that to Jordan without sounding entirely mad? Should I even try? I kenned that I did not owe him an explanation, but I kenned that, despite his gruff exterior, he did genuinely care for me like a brother. How could he possibly know how to support me if I didn't feel comfortable or safe enough to tell him what was really going on with me?

My brain, so frazzled with exhaustion, did not even make it from point A to B be with that thought process, and I simply started telling him everything.

I collapsed onto one of the benches at the kitchen table and started talking. It all poured out of me like blood gushing from an open wound. And that was also how I felt. Like my heart had been sliced open and everything was gushing out. But instead of finding some peace once it was all said and done, it still somehow was able to keep beating, mangled and mauled.

Jordan simply stared at me as I spoke. His face was expressionless. Part of me felt angry by this and wanted to stand up and poke him between the eyebrows to ask if anyone was in there. The other part could not be bothered to give a fuck, as I was all fresh out. I even found myself boarding on feeling grateful that I didn't need to explain in further detail anything more than I was already divulging.

Once I finished speaking, silence hung in the air like a toxic gas until, finally, Jordan sat down next to me and patted me on the back with a large, rough hand.

"I kenned there was sumthin' off about yer lass when I saw her the other day."

That was it. No questions, no questioning my sanity. Just a simple response. It was the first bit of sanity I had felt in almost twenty-four hours.

I was not sure if this reaction spoke to his friendship or simpleness, but truly did not give a fuss.

We sat there together in silence for a while until Jordan broke the silence again.

"Ye need a wash, my friend. Yer bowfing."

I looked over and him and gave him as much of a smile as my body could muster and said, "Aye. I guess I should go shower then, eh?"

"Aye, shoot me a text if ye need meh. I'll be around," Jordan replied.

I got up and rounded the corner into my bedroom and headed straight to the shower.

The hot water felt amazing on my body as it washed off the grime from the alleyway but stung as it hit the raw wounds on my knees and hands. I hated not being able to let the water run on my head, but I had to avoid the bandages from where the bastard had slammed the butt of his gun into my head. Twice. So, I carefully washed my face and as much of my hair as I could.

I had almost forgotten about the wound on my head. I seemed like it had been lifetimes ago after all that I had been through in the short time between then and now. The constant ache did not even serve as a reminder, as I had simply been attributing it to the emotional turmoil I was caught up in and the stress involved with trying to help Annalyse find her way back to me instead of Michael.

Once I was done showering, I walked into my room to find a visitor on my bed.

"Hello, great beast," I said as the large orange cat rolled around on my comforter, leaving a trail of cat fur in his wake. I walked over to him to give him the attention his big, fuzzy tummy demanded.

"Ah, lad. You must be hungry, aye? Let's get you some food."

I gathered the large cat into my arms and carried him up the stairs with me as I gently cooed, "Don't worry, beast, your mom *will* return to us, but until then, I will take care of ye."

After entering Annalyse's room, I put Sunshine down to free up my hands so that I could feed him. It seemed strange to still keep his stuff here in her room, when it would be better suited in the mud room or something, so I made a mental note to move the stuff after I had a nap.

As I turned to leave the room to make my way back to my own bed, I couldn't help but notice that Annalyse's Smart House Unit screen was on. Usually after a short time of not using the unit, it would revert back to its mirror like screen to go into sleep mode.

I walked over to the screen and was taken back by what I saw. It appeared as if Annalyse had been doing research on astral plane travel and had been specifically trying to learn how to connect with another soul through the plane.

My immediate thought went straight to Michael.

Why would she want to do that? I was right here. I could not wrap my mind around this. We were finally reunited. Why was she still holding onto that past life version of myself? And the pain that accompanied him. It made no sense. I ken she had gone her whole life missing him, but she found him, in me. We both felt the connection, the familiarity. I could not understand why she was doing this.

Then it hit me.

"Aine," I said uncertainly, hoping I remembered her name correctly.

"Yes, sir? I'm not used to you connecting with me through the mistress portal. Is everything ok?" she replied.

Good grief, Annalyse was right. She was very advanced. I'd never communicated with her really outside of asking for the weather, changing the temperature in the house, or ordering food.

"Um, actually, Annalyse has been injured."

I wasn't sure how much Aine kenned about Annaylse's unique situation, and that she had not really been Vivien.

"Has her soul returned to her original body?" Aine asked.

Oh shit. How did she know so much?

"Aye, it appears what way. We were attacked and Vivien's body was killed," I told her.

There was silence for a few moments, and I wondered if something had gone wrong with the unit. Just as I was about to check she said, "Good. That body was already rejecting her soul after the two of yours mated. The only way to have salvaged her soul and allow it to return to her original body was for her host body to die."

I felt like I had just been punched in the gut.

What? How could she know this? Wait....

"Is that why Annalyse was so cold and tired the next morning?" I asked.

"Yes, sir. It is."

"Aine, how do you know this?"

"Annalyse asked me to research it for her since she wasn't feeling well and could tell something was wrong, so I have been searching the internet, compiling information."

"What exactly did you find?" I inquired.

"I came across some information from ancient times about a similar situation happening. The old culture of an ancient tribe named Neimbu had believed that it was only gods who could inhabit bodies after another soul had vacated them.

This was something that was highly revered by this culture and prayed for. In this time though, what I

149

conclude is that these were not 'gods,' so to speak, but beings from other worlds that could only communicate to the people in this manner; through a recently vacated host.

They would astrally project their energy into the recently-vacated body, and used their own energy force to continue the recently vacated body's life for a short while longer. These 'spirits' brought great knowledge and taught the people many things. This is why it was seen to be a sacred and honored practice for one's body to become a host for these wise 'Knowledge Bringers.'

Other cultures saw the same phenomenon but referred to it in different ways. One refence you may be familiar with is the concept of the fallen angels from heaven who came to teach the people."

She paused for a moment to let me process what she had just shared with me. It was true, I had heard of the fallen angels, but I was not completely familiar with their story or that type of history. I had never given much energy towards looking into things like that, I felt religious documents had been doctored so much, in an effort to be used to oppress the human race, that I didn't really trust the validity of their information, so, therefore, I found it a waste of time to study their words.

"The foreign energies could only inhabit the bodies for a short amount of time before the compatibility began to wear off," she continued.

"The bodies were technically dead and the high-vibrational energy that inhabited them was very much alive, so the longer the body was used in that state, the more difficult it was for the spiritual entity to inhabit it. Once the disconnection started, the body was released to complete its journey back to Mother Earth, and the being or entity returned to its own host, realm, or reality."

I sat down on Annalyse's bed to try to keep myself from falling over.

This whole thing sounded kind of creepy to me. What Aine was telling me is that in ancient times aliens used to use recently vacated bodies as a way to teach and communicate with the people of Earth.

My tired brain was struggling to process this information and it was not finding an easy time with it. This sounded a lot like what people these days would refer to as demonic possession, and the thought of us tiptoeing so near something so dark and sinister made me feel very uncomfortable.

"Aine, did non-benevolent entities try to inhabit the bodies?" I asked.

"Yes, this is where the concept of demonic possession started. Low vibrational entities and thought forms would seek to inhabit the bodies in order to operate through them. This is when the Galactic Federation stepped in to then put an end to the ability to utilize recently vacated bodies and forbade the practice. In replacement of this communication method, what would now be considered prophets, people like Buddah and Jesus, became the next resource. These were advanced souls who entered the body as all others do, through the womb, but who regained their memories of who they truly were after they were born. Then, as humanity continued to grow and evolve, fewer prophets were needed as souls were beginning to 'wake up' at certain stages in their lives and begin remembering the truth of who they are, why they came to Earth, and their mission for humanity. These are called Starseeds.

Low vibrational entities and thought forms still attempt this behavior, though, but do so when someone is more detached from their soul through the use of recreational substances, alcohol, or poor mental health.

There is a reason alcohol is referred to as 'spirits,' and Jesus, one of the most popular spiritual teachers known, also warned against the consumption of alcohol because it opens a body up to these lower energies. The old ancient people knew the difference as they could feel the energy of that which was within the host body. The benevolent spirits brought great wisdom and teaching, the low vibrational ones just brought destruction and chaos."

Chaos.

That what exactly what was going on in my brain right now.

I could not possibly hope to assimilate or process any more information at the moment.

"Aine, I need to get some rest. Thank you for your help."

"Yes, sir."

No longer having the energy for anything else, I simply laid down on Annalyse's bed, pulled up the covers, breathed in the smell of her from her sheets, and closed my eyes in surrender, wondering what fresh hell of dreams awaited me after all I had learned today.

CHAPTER 9
Henry

Darkness.

Again.

Everything was dark.

At first, I thought I was the seed in the ground again, but this space felt much different. It did not have the warm, nurturing energy that I had experienced before. Instead, there was an emptiness here in this space. Almost as if I were in a vacuum of some sort. It was literally as if there was nothing here.

Nothing.

It was empty space.

My first instinct was to panic, but I struggled against its pull and fought to keep my fear at bay. It was challenging, but I kenned it was essential in this moment. I could be as strong as a Scottish Highland in my body, but, if I had not the strength to control my emotions, then I had no true power and was as moveable as dust being carried away in the wind. This was not a time to lose myself, as I already felt I was lost. My mind was the only thing I had in this space, and, if I lost it, I truly would be powerless. This is when I exercised true strength as a man and worked to stay in control of myself and my emotions. I forced myself to take deep breaths, as I felt my stomach twisting in knots.

Closing my eyes, I breathed.

In. Out. In. Out.

Though the view was no different with my eyes closed than it was with them opened, I still kept them shut. This sensation was familiar to me and helped me feel as if I had some control over what I was experiencing in this empty space.

Could this be where Annalyse was?

Some black abyss of nothingness?

The thought upset me and made it more challenging to control my breath, but I chose to use what could be used to destroy me as a force to fuel my fortitude and to strengthen my resolve so that I could find my way through this void. If Annalyse was here, I could only find her by staying calm and in alignment. Losing myself would help neither one of us make it through this experience.

So, I continued to breathe.

My breath was a steady metronome, constant and stable. It gave me something to focus on. Some sense of time, space, and reality in this chasm of darkness and nothingness. As I listened to my breath with my eyes closed, I came to realize that the sensation I was feeling in my stomach was not actually knots. It was that of butterflies.

But not the ones that result from nerves.

These were our *butterflies. Annalyse's and mine.*

I kept my eyes closed and continued to breathe.

I then did something I had never before thought to do, though in this moment it felt so obvious and natural. I tuned into my heart center and listened for its guidance. That is when I felt it. I felt a pull as if by some etherical cord from my sternum. I continued with my calm breathing and followed it. I did not seem to move far before I felt the tension release.

With trepidation, I slowly opened my eyes. I was surprised by what I saw – or, rather the fact that I could see. Just barely, in the darkness, I could make out the outline of light, as if it were coming through minute cracks around a door. I reached forward to see if I could find such a door, and, sure enough, my hand made contact with a handle. I attempted to turn it so that I could push the door open, but it would not budge.

Why would I have been led to a door in this dark, empty space that did not open?

I tried not to let my frustration take over. I brought my attention back to my breath and then back to my heart center. Closing my eyes, I allowed my heart to have full reign over what I felt in this space, and that is when it happened.

I could feel her.

She was on the other side of the wall.

"Annalyse," I said in a whisper, as if speaking directly to her soul.

I felt her awareness of my energy, yet the door would still not open. Part of me wanted to slam my body up against this door as many times as it took to break it down, but the other part kenned it would be no use. This was a door that she had to open, not me. So instead of trying to break down the door I decided I would simply be still, with my eyes closed and my heart open, in hopes that I could lead her to the door the same way I was led: by following my heart.

***

I woke up to light pouring over my face like a warm blanket.

Wait, shouldn't it be dark by now?

I looked around to get my bearings, having temporarily forgotten I had lain down to take a nap in Annalyse's room, and I was met with a set of large, golden eyes right in front of my face.

Sunshine was laying on my chest, staring at me.

I had not even felt the weight of his body on my chest, but realizing it was there felt soothing in some way. Part of me wondered if it was his calming energy that helped me feel safe enough to open my heart in the dark space I inhabited moments ago.

"Hello, great beast," I said, as I wrestled my arm free from the comforter, to pet his large, fluffy head. "You are a patient morning bell, aren't you? You can't possibly be hungry already though. I just fed you."

As if on cue, he let out a meow that made me question if my last statement was true.

I nudged Sunshine off to the side and moved myself into a seated position on the side of the bed.

Dear God….

My head was pounding, and my entire body ached as if Jordan and I had been clanging swords for hours the day prior and it had been a session where he had gotten in far too many blows. It seemed as if every inch of me was sore in some way.

I worked to gain my senses as my head swam from sitting up and throbbed as if someone kept knocking on it with a hammer where I had been hit with the butt of a gun hours prior.

Or was it hours?

I squinted my eyes as I peered out the window trying to take in the degree of the sun. It appeared to be too bright and fresh to be setting, but perhaps I was simply too dazed and bewildered to be a good judge.

"Aine, what time is it?" I asked.

"It is 8:34 AM, sir," she replied swiftly.

"Christ!"

The news that I had slept the rest of the day and all through the night was like a shot of adrenaline straight through to my heart.

I quickly jumped out of bed and ran down the hall and stairs.

I needed to find my phone, and fast! I could not believe I had slept the whole rest of the day and the whole night.

"Looking for this?" a familiar voice came from my kitchen.

Shannon was standing at the counter making coffee.

I stared at her dumb-struck, feeling my heart and head pound in synchronicity making me feel as if I may collapse.

"Want some?" she asked.

Coffee sounded wonderful. The thought of the heat and caffeine gave me hope that I may be able to find a clear head, and soon.

"Aye," I said. "But what are you doing here? How is Annalyse? I have to go to her."

"Why?" she said as if she thought I was being melodramatic. "She's not going anywhere, and besides, Morgan is with her. I stayed until she arrived last night, and she told me she had the day off today and would be spending the night."

She reached out the cup of coffee towards me. "I don't know how you take it," she said with a slight shrug.

I took the coffee mug from her and walked with it slowly over to the refrigerator. After adding some coconut milk creamer to it, I walked over to the table and sat down on the bench nearest to the kitchen to face Shannon.

I took a long sip of coffee then looked up at Shannon and said, "I can not believe I slept so long."

"You can't? You've been up all night and suffered a severe trauma. You're healing too. Of course you're tired."

I hadn't really looked at it that way until now.

It is difficult, as a man, to see myself as any type of victim. Especially a large, strong man as myself. Something I learned from Annalyse though, was that healing started when we finally admit to ourselves what happened and begin to face and acknowledge the effect that it had on us.

That was almost harder than suffering and experiencing the actual event.

I simply looked at Shannon and nodded, unsure how to navigate that territory. This was a new space I was entering into, and I felt lost and exposed – vulnerable even – and I did not like it.

We sat in silence for a few minutes, sipping on our hot coffees and simply being still. Then Shannon broke the silence.

"She still loves you, you know?"

What an odd thing to say, I thought.

"Aye," I said with a nod. I thought for a minute and then suddenly remembered the strange dream I had whilst I was asleep last night.

"Shannon, I learned, once getting home, that Annalyse had been utilizing our Smart Home device to help her research astral travel. She was trying to learn how to connect with another spirit, intentionally, through the astral plane." I paused for a moment because I did not want to share the rest due to embarrassment and hurt, but I kenned it was important to be open if I was going to work through my troubles and be stronger on the other side.

"I think she was deliberately trying to find Michael."

I always felt strange talking about myself in that way. Though I do not fully remember my life as Michael, I remember enough to find it odd to refer to myself as someone else entirely.

"That makes sense to me, Henry. Her soul was being pulled to that version of yourself for some reason or another. There is some type of unfinished business there that needed to be brought into balance."

"I hadn't really thought of it that way. I'd simply thought she was unhappy with me and just wanted to be with him."

That was the first time I had said that out loud, and I could almost feel the sense of relief as I spoke the words, even though I could feel heat rising in my face after saying them. It was a heavy weight I had been carrying, and I did not realize how heavy until I got them off my chest.

Shannon's response was not at all what I was expecting.

"Look Henry, I'm going to be real with you. This," she waved her arms around in front of me, "has got to stop. You are not some victim in this. Yes, you have experienced a trauma, and you have every right to need time to cope, but you aren't even focused on that. You're focused on the fact that Annalyse isn't doing what you want her to do, and you're acting as if this makes you a victim of some sort. You're wearing your victimhood like some gawdy badge of honor or something.

Annalyse has not *done* anything to you. The universe hasn't done something to you. You chose this path before you even incarnated here. So did she. This is what you need to understand. Yes, you experienced trauma, but so did she. She was sexually assaulted and murdered. Give her spirit the time it needs to heal from this, and if she needs to do that level of healing with you as the version of yourself that she is more familiar with, let her do it. Can't you see through this haze of yours enough to understand?

She had to have a choice. She had to be able to choose if she would walk this path after what happened to her and what she experienced. If she had been forced to carry this cross without having the ability to choose it, then she would have resented it and there would never be the healing that needs to occur. It is in the choice where she is able to stand in her power. You cannot deny her that, Henry, and how dare you try. Your journey is one and the same. Allow her to do her part, and instead of trying to control her by making her do what you want her to do, focus your energy on doing yours.

Have you even processed what happened to *you* and what you had to endure? What you had to witness? Or have you been so focused on 'fixing' the 'problem' with Annalyse that you have put your own mental health and wellbeing on the backburner? You're no good to her when you refuse to process your own trauma and heal your own shit.

Just because you don't process it doesn't mean it goes away. It stays stored in your unconscious mind, warping and effecting every choice and decision you make. How could you possibly be the man that she will need when she comes back if you are still operating from an unconscious, wounded place? How will you be able to step up and walk this journey with her if you're refusing to do the work?

Stop fixating on what Annalyse is doing. If she chose to cross over, she would have by now. She didn't and she hasn't and she won't, and at some level you *know* this to be true, but you're choosing to fixate on it because it gives you an excuse not to go inward and heal your own stuff. This is the typical stuff men do. Instead of healing their own stuff, they fixate on trying to fix the problems of everyone else as a way of thinking they are balancing the scales.

Let me tell you: you are not. You're only feeding your own wound that you have come here to heal. Just as Annalyse has her Witch's Wound, you have your Warrior's Wound; the wound men unconsciously carry as perpetrators of the oppression to the Divine Feminine.

This is why you want to fix her problems instead of healing your own shit.

On an unconscious level, men think they can pay their penance for what the masculine energy was responsible for and the atrocities it placed upon the feminine by trapping all of their pain inside and 'fixing' the energy that they "broke."

It doesn't work that way. Both must do the work to heal. She is working to heal her wound. Let her. And in the process, you work to heal your own. It is a heavy burden to come into this life with every stored memory of every act you have ever made against the feminine in all your lifetimes.

This needs to be healed too, otherwise you will continue the cycle of hurting one another through your unconscious behaviors. Hers, to try to keep herself safe, and yours to try to control her in order for your ego to feel you have succeeded in finally paying your "debt" – or even more foolishly to think that by controlling her you will keep her safe. Her journey is not one for you to dictate or control. It is her own."

Shannon may as well have hit me with a tranquilizer dart that was laced with some toxic acid.

I sat there frozen as each of her words ate at me like a flesh-eating bacteria.

She squatted down in front of me and added, "Look, I'm sorry. I know that was probably difficult to hear, but it needed to be said. I'm here to help you, and you need a reality check. You're so focused on yourself that you're not seeing the whole picture. You're not seeing her, Henry. And you're not seeing yourself. You're seeing a problem that doesn't exist, but only in your mind, as a distraction from your true pain."

"Difficult to hear," was an understatement. I could have thought of many things more pleasant to do than listen to her abrasive words cutting through me like tiny shards of glass.

Of course, she was right.

I had been so focused on just wanting her to wake up and being back with me that I had not even seen the situation through her perspective.

Fuck.

I looked up at Shannon, and, only because she looked wobbly and blurry, had I just noticed that I had started tearing up.

"I can't see her. She won't let me."

"What do you mean?" she asked compassionately as she sat down on the bench next to me.

"I had a dream about her last night. I was in a completely dark space. I couldn't see anything, but I could feel her here," I pointed at the middle of my chest. "I followed the feeling, and it led me to a door. When I tried to go in, I could not. It was locked. I tried calling to her, but it did nothing. It was not until I sent energy from my heart center that I felt a response from her. The door never opened though."

Shannon was silent for quite some time until my patience got the better of me. She would do this sometimes, as if she were gathering information from some ethereal source that I could not access, and it frustrated me as if I were being left out of some secret knowledge.

"What is it, Shannon?" I asked, working to keep my tone level and respectful.

"You went into The Void last night," she said slowly as she looked straight ahead at nothing in particular.

"What do you mean?"

"It means," she began as she looked back at me. "That the two of you are in complete separation right now. I hadn't realized the separation was so severe. Her trauma must be very deep. She is not just healing from what just happened to her, she's healing timelines and generations of trauma by going in that deep." Gently placing a hand on mine she added, "I am getting a better handle on your level of pain. I do understand now that your pain must indeed be rather intolerable. To be separated from one's own soul…." Her worlds trailed of.

I understood why.

There *were* no words for this level of pain.

So, I said nothing, as again, there were no words necessary.

We were silent for several minutes until she went on.

"You need to do your work now, Henry. While there is separation. I do not mean to rush you, but this is important."

"Why?"

"Because there is no interference from her energy. That must be why she needed to be completely separated from yours."

Her gaze wandered off again as if she was looking at nothing, and I decided to let her hear whatever it was she was being told.

We sat there, again in silence, for a little while longer before she turned to look at me with a very serious expression on her face.

"Henry, are you truly serious about going in and getting her?"

I sat straight up and said, "I would do whatever it takes."

"Good," she said. "Because it's not her you're going to need to connect with in order to get to her. You're going to have to connect with Michael."

"What? I do not ken what you mean. Why would I need to connect with him?"

"Because that's the only part of your soul that you're still in union with. He is you. Just from a different timeline. You can find her that way."

My brain computed her words like an ancient computer, slowly filing and processing the new information it was given. Once it all painstakingly locked into its designated place and integrated into my whole thought process, I realized the validity in what she was saying.

"Aye," I said. "But, Shannon, how? How do I connect with an old timeline version of myself in a way that I can reach her where she is?"

Shannon took a deep breath and stood up. She then held out her hand in offering to me. I took it and stood up.

"Let's go, Henry. It's time to do some Shadow Work."

CHAPTER 10

Henry

"Shannon, what the hell is shadow work?" I asked as she was getting me to lay down on my bed.

I felt uncomfortable laying down in my bed with her in my bedroom. It seemed inappropriate and disrespectful to Annalyse. I took a deep breath and reminded myself that I was laying down to help Annalyse, and Shannon was here to help both of us, and that nothing scandalous was going on or was about to happen.

"Shadow work," she said as she brought over a chair from the sitting area over by the fireplace and placed it next to my bed. "Is the process of coming to terms with your 'shadow' self."

This does not sound fun, I thought.

Lying flat on my back, I turned my head to look at her with a quizzically raised eyebrow.

She sat down and began to explain, "One's 'shadow' is that part of them that they do not like. Therefore they keep it suppressed, as if there is something evil or dirty about it. In truth, the shadow self is really the collection of trauma residue trapped in someone's energy field." She paused for a second when she sat down to make herself comfortable. "See, all 'dark' energy is the result of some type of trauma or wounding. It doesn't even have to have occurred in this lifetime, either. 'Evil' or 'bad' people typically become that way as a result of some type of childhood trauma or activating event that triggers a past lifetime wound. This presents as a shadow aspect or archetype.

The irony is that so many people think it's their deepest, darkest self, when, in fact, it's the residual energy left over from trying to protect oneself from being vulnerable after having suffered at the hands of another in their past or doing a wrong to another as a perpetrator and wishing to undo it by simply denying it and trying to act like it never happened. Both the Witch's Wound and the Warrior's Wound would be considered part of one's 'shadow,' and, the more suppressed they are, the more they tend to negatively impact one's behavior or experience here in their current lifetime. The suppression feeds the wound; the acceptance and processing of it unlock the hidden parts within us that need to be integrated into the whole, in order for us to step into our true self and full power.

It is the process of suppression that causes the thoughtform to become toxic – not the memory itself. So many people walk around with what they feel are grotesque secrets about their experience that either they have done or that have been done to them, so they suppress this version of themselves, pushing it down deep, hoping no one will see it. To do shadow work is to face your shadow and show it the love, compassion, and acceptance that it didn't receive in the time that it was created. This helps it integrate into the whole.

This is also why so many people go through life feeling a sort of emptiness. It is because they have many pieces that they are refusing to integrate, since they feel it will be too painful to process and release them. Unfortunately, the only way out is through, as they say, so there really isn't any other option. Fortunately, if the work is done correctly and well, it typically turns out like that children's book *The Monster At The End Of This Book,* where one comes to realize that the biggest thing they actually feared was their self. Becoming the version of one's self that is no longer aligned with the perpetrator/victim energy and becoming one's true expression is a terrifying thought to many. There are too many unknowns.

Doing this work means letting go of so many false beliefs that people have built their entire experience on. Without those beliefs they feel they will have completely lost their identity, when, in fact, the opposite is true: they will have finally found it.

This is what we are going to do now, Henry. We are going to work to fully integrate you with your true self so that you can align completely with your higher self. By doing this, you will be able to tap into Michael's energy and connect with Annalyse. But, like I said, the only way out is through, so it's time to face your shadow and integrate yourself completely."

Well shit....

I could tell where this was going, and I could already feel memories attempting to bubble up from a deep pit that would have been my emotional equivalent to The Mariana Trench. I gulped hard as if to push them further down and prevent them from coming up out of my mouth. It felt like swallowing a rock.

I sat up and looked at Shannon and said, "I do not want to do this."

I felt my heart beginning to race. My nervous system was on fire with the urge to run. Shannon may as well have been a deadly dragon about to burn me alive, as the threat she presented seemed just as strong. In truth, I would rather be at the end of a dragon's breath and be burned alive than to be consumed by my own emotions, at the mercy of my past actions.

She simply looked at me with compassion and said, "I know, but are you willing to face your darkness in order to be able to find Annalyse?"

If there was anyone or anything I would go up against such a dragon for, it was my beloved Anam Faileas, Annalyse, but why did it have to be this way? I would battle a thousand dragons, walk across hot coals, or drag my naked body across a field of glass for Annalyse... but this?

I truly felt that this would be one of the most difficult things I had ever done and would ever do.

Once I got over the initial moment of wanting to resist the inevitable, I realized that this is what women must feel like when they are about to give birth. They do not want to do it, but they have no choice. It is happening whether they want it to or not. And now it was my turn to birth something new. A new version of myself. It was time for me to become the full expression of what I was created to be and move fully into the light.

"Wait." I said suddenly as what Shannon had just said, and my own thoughts, had finally solved an equation that I did not ken needed solving. "Are you trying to tell me that the reason I couldn't see in that dark space was because of my 'shadow?'"

"That's what I'm getting, Henry," she said. "Annalyse is in a very special and high vibrational place where she is doing a lot of healing work with you as the version she has known this whole, current life experience: Michael. Her soul has been touched by him long before she felt the touch of your hand on her skin. It makes sense that she needs to heal with him, and, if you want to be able to get into that space, you need to be able to bring your shadow into the light."

Fuck.

I kenned exactly what experience of mine I associated with the "darkness" in me, and mine was not so much brought on by a trauma caused by another; the trauma was caused by me. It was not something I set out to do or meant to do, but it still happened at my hands, and I have carried the weight of that burden very, very deep within me, working relentlessly to not give it a foothold to ever surface in my mind. Now Shannon wanted me to deliberately bring it forth, think of it, and share it with another.

Dear God, help me.

I looked at her imploringly, as if to ask with my eyes one last time if this was something I truly must do and was met with a matter-of-fact nod. So I simply surrendered, laid back down, and took a deep, shaky breath.

"It's already surfacing isn't it?" Shannon asked.

Christ! How did she always ken everything?

"Aye," I said while staring at the ceiling, hoping it would keep the images out of my mind. It was easy for it to begin rising to my conscious awareness. I was emotionally raw and had been recently traumatized. It was as if whatever tear had been made by my recent trauma made a gap for other pains to escape through.

"Well close your eyes and let's face it together."

I looked over at her again, the movement causing a tear that had just blossomed from my eye to roll down the side of my cheek.

"Please do not judge me, Shannon. I'm not that man anymore."

"I know," she said. "And I'm not here to cast judgment. I'm here to hold space for you and Annalyse so that you can complete your mission. You may not be that man anymore, Henry, but by holding on to that shadow version of him, you're still carrying the weight of him. It's time to integrate that man into who you are today and allow him to find rest and peace."

I nodded my head as I turned my face back towards the ceiling then closed my eyes, forcing more tears to fall down the sides of my face.

"Take a few deep breaths," Shannon instructed as she began guiding me into a more hypnotic state. "Now, I want you to imagine a white light hovering right above your head. This light is absolute love. Allow that light to flow through the top of your head, feel it as it slowly passes behind your eyes, down into your throat, filling you with love. Now, feel it as it flows deeper into your chest, down into your solar plexus and into your abdomen. Feel its warmth and comfort there. Now, allow it to flow all the way down into your tailbone and feel it continue down into the earth. In your mind's eye, see that it makes deep, strong roots into the earth. You can now feel Mother Earth sending her loving, warm energy up this cord and into your spine, all the way up to the top of your head.

Take a few more deep breaths as you feel all this warm, loving energy circling through your body like a battery circuit.

Now, I want you to imagine that you're sitting in a private movie theater, and, on the big screen, you are going to see the event begin playing out just like a movie – that was the source of your shadow. Tell me what you see."

I took a deep breath and spoke very calmly, "I see myself as a much younger man. I had just begun University, and I am at a party. We are all drinking a lot. I see a young woman whose name was Susan. I had been watching her most of the evening. I like her, but never had the nerve to ask her out. With both our minds well lubricated with alcohol, I decide this was my chance to make my move. I approach her and we begin talking. I am able to convince her to go somewhere more private." I could feel more tears again as they made their way down the sides of my face.

"She was very drunk, and we had sex. I felt this was the only way that counted as success with her. It was not enough for her to accept a date with me or to get a kiss. I truly believed that having sex with her was the way I won her. She barely moved or said anything, and it only lasted a few moments."

It was difficult for me to talk about this as this had always been a moment in my life that I had not been proud of, and after meeting Annalyse and hearing of her experiences and knowing the pain they caused her, it had carved the trench even deeper where I kept this particular memory hidden.

"What happens next, Henry?"

"A few days go by, and I see Susan on campus and smile at her thinking things had changed between us and that since having sex it would make her more attached to me and that we were on our way to becoming an item. But she does not return the smile. Instead, she looks angry or even afraid of me. I did not understand why. I kenned I had not hurt her in any way and she was physically fine. I could not wrap my mind around why she would be having feelings like that towards me.

Months went by and her behavior seemed to shift dramatically. She dressed more conservatively, and she had cut off all her beautiful, blonde hair. I figured she just had a lot of stress from school or something, and, since we never spoke, I could never get any real answers from her. Until one day when she came up behind me and asked if she could have a word with me.

I was thrilled, thinking this was my chance to pick up where we had left off, but I was horribly wrong. She told me that when we had sex, I had gotten her pregnant, and, when her parents found out, after she was no longer able to hide it from them, they forced her to have an abortion, even though she was several months along. She went on to tell me that the abortion procedure, as painful as it was, apparently had not gotten everything because a few days after, she miscarried the remains of the fetus into her bathtub while she was trying to get some relief from the cramps she was experiencing due to the procedure.

Susan then shoved something at me, placing it on my chest, and said, 'This is what I found in my bath water. Next time you decide to have sex with someone without their consent, you should really at least wear a condom. I truly wish we could have traded places in that bathtub, so you could have gotten a glimpse of the pain you've put me through, all for an orgasm and a conquest. Women were not created just to be a man's masturbation tool, and there can be unforeseen consequences that the women get stuck with. Learn to take responsibility for prevention – especially if you can't control yourself. That shouldn't just be a burden thrust upon women.'

I watched her in shock as she walked away. It took me a moment to realize that what she had shoved at me was a polaroid picture. When I looked at it, it took me a few moments to realize what it was that I was seeing. The picture contained her hand and in it was what looked like globs of blood, but when I looked closer at the image, I could see what looked like a tiny hand.

She had given me a picture of the remaining fragments of our child."

Tears now streamed from my eyes as I recounted this horrific memory. I had thrown the picture away almost immediately after realizing what it was, hoping that in some way it would get rid of what I had seen, but the image was seared into my brain for life, and I have worked very hard to not see it.

It was difficult to speak through the tears, but I managed to say, "I never had imagined that just some drunken sex could possibly ever have resulted in a scenario that scarred that young woman so severely. What happened as a result of my actions will be with Susan her entire life. It will affect her every time she thinks of having sex and replays the possible consequences and associated trauma. It will affect her when it comes to dating or trusting other men. In one night, just for sex and my ego, I very well may have stolen that woman's dreams of being married and having a family. Within a few moments, I stole a version of Susan's life from her that she would mourn the loss of for the rest of her days."

"Yes, Henry," Shannon began, "to you it was just sex, but to her it became a nightmare where she played what she felt was the villain, and then had to witness the result of that role firsthand."

I nodded in agreement as the tears continued to pour down my cheeks.

"Henry, you need to forgive yourself."

With my eyes still closed, my mind's eye was still fixed on the image of that version of myself who had so selfishly ruined that young woman's life. She had once been this vibrant, laughing, gorgeous, magical creature, but before the semester was through, she had gained weight, lost her luster, and ended up dropping out of school, and I was the one responsible.

"Shannon, how can I forgive myself for what I did?"

"Maybe you can't. Maybe you just have to be open to forgiveness and allow the universe to forgive him through you. Go to him and embrace him. Tell him you learned from that situation. Tell him it made you a better man. Tell him it allowed you to have grace and compassion for Annalyse when you two came into union in this lifetime. Tell him that you are balancing your karma, and thank him for his role in your journey. Tell him you know he didn't mean any harm, and that, at his core, you know him to be a good man."

"How can I possibly deserve forgiveness for what I did?"

"Because you are human, and you are divine. Focus on the part of you that is God. Is that part worthy of forgiveness?"

"Aye, but what about her? How can I just let go of this burden and lay it down, knowing she may still carry it?"

"By laying it down, you are breaking the energetic bond that connects you two. What's done is done and you cannot un-ring a bell. Once the trauma has occurred to each spirit – and yes the perpetrator's spirit does get traumatized by the act of going against another human – the healing is up to each individual. You cannot fix, make better, or erase what you did by tormenting yourself. You have to let it go so that the energy can be transmuted and transcended into something new that benefits living kind, instead of holding it in a repeating, vibrational pattern of suffering. Energy can neither be created or destroyed, only changed. Change the energy, Henry. Allow it. Do it for you. Do it for Susan. Do it for Annalyse. Do it for the collective."

After Shannon finished speaking, I surrendered and did as she advised. In my mind's eye, I approached the young man I had once been, who had just looked at the picture that had been thrust at him and said, "*Hello, lad. I am so sorry I could not be there for you before this happened to build up your confidence and teach you what it truly means to be a man and to understand where your true worth comes from. I am so sorry that you have suffered alone, under the weight of what happened, and I was never there for you to help you process it. I am so sorry that I shunned you and only fed into the shame and sorrow you felt as a result of what happened.*"

I stepped forward and embraced him before continuing.

"*I forgive you. I ken you did not mean any harm. I ken your heart and know that truly you are a good man. I ken that if you saw a man attempting to assault a woman, you would step in and do what is right.*" *I pulled back to look at him while keeping my hands on his shoulders and said, "You no longer have to carry this weight and I free you from it. This is now my burden to bear.*"

In that moment that version of me dissolved into golden dust and began floating away in the wind. As I watched the energy particles float away, I said, "I allow this energy that was once caused to make pain to now be transmuted and transformed into that which will serve the highest good of the collective. I lay my burden on the alter of the universe and present it as new and potential energy to be used for good."

At one point I wondered if I could drown in my own tears.

They would not stop coming.

It was like a spring rain, washing away and cleansing all the surfaces of their pollen, but instead of something life giving, what I was washing away was death and soul-sucking. The tears were uncomfortable, but I allowed them, knowing their cleansing properties.

"Ok, Henry, it's time to come back to the present," Shannon said, breaking through the sounds of my sobs. "I'm going to count down from five and when I do, I want you to open your eyes. Five, four, three, two, one. You may open your eyes."

I opened them and stared up at the ceiling before sitting up and moving myself so that I was seated on the edge of my bed. I looked at Shannon and could see that she too had tears running down her cheeks.

"Forgive me," I said. "I ken that must have been a painful story to have heard."

Shaking her head slightly she replied, "It's not that."

"What is it?" I asked.

Letting out a small puff of a laugh, as she looked off into the distance at nothing in particular, she said, "Through this journey, I have known deep in my bones that I was meant to help you and Annalyse. I knew I was to assist in the healing that needed to take place. It's ironic, though," turning her face to look at me, she gave a half smile before continuing, "I hadn't imagined that you would help me with mine."

I stared at her for a moment in confusion before saying, "I am sorry, Shannon. I do not ken your meaning."

Shannon then went on to explain, "I too had a similar experience to Susan's, and, by witnessing you and your heartache over the whole situation, just now, it actually brought me healing by having the opportunity to witness your pain while I was in a position to extend compassion and empathy. Thank you."

I pondered her words for a few moments as I stared at my interlaced fingers resting in my lap before looking back up at her.

"You're welcome," I said as more tears began to come as a result of what she just shared with me.

Shannon then stood up, embraced me, and whispered, "I forgive you, too."

I kenned that, in that moment she was representing Susan for me, and I represented the man who had impregnated her, and together we wept and healed. It was one of those surreal moments where in a million years I could never have imagined the universe bringing this to pass, but alas, here it was.

It was then that I truly understood that, even through pain, the universe was always conspiring in my favor. Life feels so long to us, but, in truth, as endless beings it is such a short adventure. I really began to contemplate whether everything really had been preplanned before we incarnated into each lifetime and if we made those soul contracts with others in order for us to all act out experiences that one another needed for their own soul's evolution and growth.

It was in this moment that I believed that to be true. What were the odds that Shannon and I would come together like this, in this time and space, to allow an open space for each other's unique wound to be healed? This was no coincidence. This was meant to be. Just like Annalyse and I were meant to be.

I pulled back from the hug and looked Shannon square in the eyes and said, "I'm ready to go back in."

"Are you sure?" Shannon asked, while looking at me with uncertainty. Or was that concern? "You have just processed a massive trauma. I'm not sure now is the right time."

"Aye, I am sure," I said with confidence.

"Help me understand where you are in your thinking," she said, obviously not convinced.

"I see now. The wounding. I get it. I ken now why I could not see in that space with the doors. It was because I did not want to see. What I am realizing is there were many other doors in that space, many of which contained things that I have suppressed and have not been willing to accept, face, or embrace. This is why I could not see the doors. It is because, for so long, I did not want to see them, so I pushed them into a deep, dark corner of my mind where I could hide them away and not have to deal with them. This must also be the space where I buried the trauma from when Annalyse and I first split apart in our origination story, and it sounds

191

like the only way to access that information is to go deeper into this shadow space."

As I spoke, I could see the understanding slowly begin to re-sculpt her features, as she leaned back, absorbing all the new information I was giving her.

"I ken how to get to her now, but I must find a way to create a safe space for her to come to me."

We sat together in silence for a while as I contemplated my options. I had not realized Shannon's position on my discovery until she interrupted my planning.

"Henry, I think you're going about this is the wrong way."

God help me with this woman. I truly appreciated her role in my journey and in this process, but I was getting tired of her constant pushback. It was tiresome.

"Aye? And why is that?" I asked, trying to contain my frustration.

I was finally feeling like I was making progress and headway, and here she is throwing roadblocks in my way.

"It was your verbiage just a few moments ago."

I stared at her in a way that I assumed made it obvious that I needed more information from her.

"You said that you had to make her 'come' to you," she began. "This tells me you're still missing the important fact that she is you, like you are her. It's not a thing of getting her to 'come' to you. It's about you tuning into that vibration that is her. That *is* you. The energy that is the two of you in union together. When you can simply tune into that, you will find her."

I laid back down on the bed and stared at the ceiling while I processed the information Shannon just gave me. Shannon might be to me what the American's call a "party pooper," but she always seems to come in with a valid point each time. I did not like how much that bothered me on a deep level. It ticked at my annoyance level strongly.

Closing my eyes, I allowed myself to take in a few deep breaths. I kenned what she was saying. It was not that I need to create a safe space for Annalyse. It was that I needed to feel safe myself. The safe space was for me. This whole thing reminded me of the concept of someone being afraid of the dark. It was not the dark that was scary, it was those things lying beyond our conception that terrified us. It is that fear of the unknown that cripples us. The irony lies in the fact that, typically, when we finally do get up the courage to shine light into the darkest corners, we very rarely reveal a monster, but, instead, a small, terrified, wounded animal that simply needs to be loved and accepted.

In this moment I felt like one of those poor, wretched creatures myself. I was exhausted, both mentally and physically, because I was fighting a battle I could not win. It was as if I was trying to wage war against the forces that cause the earth to spin on her axis. I was powerless to resist, but yet I fought and warred against this in some hope of asserting control over it.

Ah, the same struggle all who work from the imbalanced masculine energy struggle with. It is like some primal need that almost feels as if it could consume me. I must assert control, and if I cannot then I will focus all my energy on trying to.

Dear God, the pain and suffering this causes. I could not quite understand why it was so difficult for me to just let go and to just allow these things to unfold the way they were meant to while I just stay open and willing to fulfill my role. Fear and the need to assert control seem to go hand in hand.

I took another deep breath and stared at the ceiling some more, unclear on what else to do.

CHAPTER 11
Henry

Shannon refused to help me further with my efforts to go in to try to find Annalyse until I spent some time taking care of myself and processing my own trauma. As much as I hated admitting it to her, I detested her for it. I felt as if she was keeping from me the one thing I desired most.

I kenned, from a more balanced perspective, that she, of course, was right, but it did not mean that I liked it or felt good about the decision. Several weeks had gone by without seeing her yet nothing had changed.

The Christmas and New Year holidays came and went with barely any recognition on my part. It mattered not to me what others wanted to celebrate. Without Annalyse with me, there was nothing worth celebrating. Not a Christ child nor a New Year.

There was nothing, nothing at all.

I spent as much time as possible with Annalyse at the hospital and would see Morgan as we would trade out who would stay with her and when. My life was consumed with the grey sterile walls of my prison that was this godforsaken hospital, sitting by Annalyse's bed holding her hand, and sleeping when I could.

My physical body had all but healed, yet I felt as if my emotional wounds were being carved deeper and deeper the longer I had to wait for my neach-gaoil.

The longer I went without being with Annalyse, the more my feelings become like the edge of an echo that no longer brings satisfaction but only the pain of loss and the reminder of what was... what could have been but is not. It was like I was back to loving the ghost of my lover whom I had never been quite sure had even existed. Even though she was here, right in front of me, Annalyse was a million miles away where I could not reach her and was becoming just as fabled to me now as she used to be before we reunited.

This did something to a man.

God – I had already thought I had been broken enough to be completely undone, but here I had no peace. There was no rest. No closure. I could not mourn the loss of someone living right in front of me. How could I? It was an impossible road to navigate. How do you mourn the loss of a phantom without becoming one yourself?

My love, oh so real, was yet also becoming an echo of what it once was. It was as if the light inside me was slowly going out, and all I had to hold on to was the remains of melted wax slipping through my fingers.

We were both becoming echoes. The whisper of a memory still just beyond our grasp.

The days all blended together, and time no longer mattered to me. It was irrelevant.

Time did not exist in hell.

Today was like any other day that I had stayed the night with Annalyse. The sun rose and shone through the window. I could tell it was cold outside by the small remnants of frost decorating the outside of the window, as if it had been painted by frost fairies in the night.

January was always rather cold in Virginia as Virginia's weather goes. January and February were always the coldest and seemed right in alignment with the winters I had experienced as a child in Scotland.

As the sun rose, so did I.

I began my regular routine of massaging Annalyse's limbs and helping to flex each of the joints. I would always start with her fingers, carefully move my way up her arms as I navigated past the tubes still connected to her, and then work from her toes up her legs. I was always so nervous and careful, as I was afraid to disturb her feeding tube or cause her any pain.

The nurses said they could do these things for her, but I wanted to. It was a way for me to feel like I was doing something for her. It was a tangible way for me to help her. Morgan had taken the task of helping to bathe Annalyse, as I felt it inappropriate. I had never seen her naked in this body and I felt that it would be best, the first time that happens, for her to be fully aware and a willing participant to consent.

As I was working my way up Annalyse's second leg, Morgan entered the room, her arms filled with a few different types of bags.

"Good morning," she said as she walked into the room. "I brought bagels and coffee," she added as she lifted her packages slightly as if gesturing to them.

That was nice of her, I thought.

I had not connected much with Morgan over the last few weeks, and she had been kind enough to not push me into talking or connecting in any way. Most of our exchanges were simple and shallow. Random remarks about the weather, asking if things had changed – though we kenned they had not.

The only time Morgan veered off the typical shallow exchanges was a few days before Christmas Holiday. She had invited me to take a few hours and join her and her husband for their Yule dinner, but the idea of even attempting to wish someone a cantie Yule seemed far too great a challenge for the likes of me. How, without the strength of God himself, could I bring myself to attempt to celebrate the holiday, or anything for that matter? There was nothing of it but to turn her invitation down.

I appreciated her kindness toward me.

"Thank you," I said as I continued gently massaging Annalyse's leg.

Seeing the bagels made me realize that it had been days since I had last eaten, and something went off in my head like a light bulb that just popped out, with its last sudden burst of an attempt to lengthen its purpose of shining.

As I massaged Annalyse's leg, I noticed how thin she was beginning to look. Yes, she was being fed, but she was only consuming food through a feeding tube, and, because she was not able to move around as she was used to, her muscles had begun deteriorating.

I too was becoming thinner, looking less like myself and more like a shell of my former self. Could Annalyse and I truly be so connected on a deep level that what was happening in, with, and to her body even had an effect on mine?

I must have gotten very caught up in my thoughts because I had just become aware of someone saying my name.

"Henry. *Henry*..."

I looked up to see Morgan staring at me as if she had been searching for me inside the deep cave that had become my mind.

"Aye?" I answered as I slowly lowered Annalyse's leg back down to the bed.

"I was just asking what kind of bagel you'd like," Morgan answered, looking concerned.

"Oh, I do not think I will have one." I said before quickly adding, "Thank you, though" due to the look on her face.

Morgan narrowed her eyes at me and said, "Plain, it is."

As I walked around the bed to come closer to her she added, "And don't even try it. You look like shit and I have been nice, but this is ridiculous." She shoved a plain bagel in my face that she had been smearing with cream cheese while chastising me, then added, "Now eat the goddamn bagel."

In this moment, I wanted to take back the mental narrative about her kindness that I had just had with myself prior to her showing up, but I had to admit that she had a point.

Could my theory be probable?

Could Annalyse and I be so connected that what was happening to our bodies affected the other? If they were, by my neglecting caring for myself I was also weakening Annalyse. There was a part of me that wanted to slide into the self-pity parade as the main event, but the way Annalyse's bones felt under my touch a few moments prior halted my arrival.

I took the bagel and began chewing it.

It was not until I had hit my tongue that my whole body reminded me of how much I had been punishing it, more like punishing myself – by not eating. My stomach growled and my mouth began to heavily salivate in its attempt to welcome something that would provide it temporary satiation.

Morgan then patted me on the shoulder and said, "Good boy" before walking over to sit down next to Annalyse.

"How is she?" she asked.

I had to quickly chew and swallow to answer her.

I walked over to stand next to her and laid a hand on Annalyse's before answering.

"The same. Nothing has changed except she just seems to be getting thinner," I said before finishing the sentence in my head. *But that is going to change soon....*

I had a renewed sense of purpose and drive beginning to course through my veins.

If my theory had even the remotest possibility of being true, then I must do everything I could to stand in the gap for Annalyse.

Morgan let out a deep sigh in response to my answer and said nothing else.

I decided, since she was here and now I had an idea on a new way that I could support Annalyse, I would go ahead and leave Annalyse in Morgan's care.

"Thank you for being here with her, Morgan," I said as I grabbed my coat off the cot in the room. "I think I will be headed home now that I know she is in such good hands."

"No problem," she said. Then looking over her shoulder to look at me added, "And Henry?"

"Aye?" I asked, just as I was headed out the door.

"Make sure you take a shower."

I let out a small laugh in response, grabbed another bagel, gave her a small nod and smile, and then walked out the door.

God, it was freezing outside.

I was glad to get into my vehicle and turn the heat on full blast. I took a moment and looked at myself in the rearview mirror and was almost startled at what I saw.

I looked ill.

My skin looked dry and more lined. My eyes even looked dull and bloodshot.

I took a deep breath and settled into my resolve.

"Annalyse doesn't want to look at some half dead looking zombie when she wakes up. She's going to want to see the Henry she kenned, and it's time we bring him back," I said to the face staring back at me.

I took another deep breath, put my car in reverse, and made my way back home.

When I got home, I decided to check the mailbox for mail and was astounded to see it almost completely full up with parcels and letters.

"Christ," I said as I worked to unload the collection of junk mail and bills into my lap.

Looking at this pile of unattended to mess in my lap made me feel as if I were looking at a paper version of my own brain. So many things unsorted and unprocessed just jumbled together in a big muddle.

Well, no more.

After getting the mess into the house, I laid it all out on the counter to start sorting through it.

It was all pretty standard stuff – bills, credit offers that would end up in the shredder, random offers by local companies.

I tore into my cable bill and was shocked by the number I saw. It was almost double what I was used to seeing.

"What in the hell?" I said as I unfolded the statement.

There was a late fee caused by my neglect and another charge that accounted for the difference.

When my eyes rested on the line that explained the extra, my heart began thumping, and I could feel rage building in my body as if I were being caught on fire from the inside out.

I stormed out of the kitchen, out the side doors, and made my way over to the garage where Jordan lived above our exercise facility.

"JORDAN!" I thundered as I burst through the door into the building. I had caught him in the middle of working out.

"JORDAN! WHAT IN THE ACTUAL FUCK IS THIS GARBAGE DOING ON MY CABLE BILL?" I roared at him.

"What are ye on about?" he asked looking confused.

"THIS!" I said, as I shoved the cable bill in his face.

He fumbled with the bill for a moment as he worked to see what it said then responded with a shrug, "So? I had a chug. I dunna ken why yer all crabbit about it."

"You do not ken?" I asked, as I glowered down over him while he sat down on a nearby bench to wipe sweat off his face.

He just looked up at me with a shrug, as if I were out of my mind.

"Jordan, it is this kind of shit that make men see women as sex objects. It is this SHIT" I spat as I pointed at the line on the bill, "that makes men think that women are things to be objectified. This goddamn garbage is what feeds the trafficking industry because a pig like you thinks it's no big deal! IT IS A BIG, FUCKING DEAL!"

My throat hurt from yelling so loudly, and my entire body was shaking as my breaths heaved in my chest. Jordan just stared at me like I was some type of electrical explosion he wished he could get away from, but knew trying to flee would only put him in more danger.

"Do you really not get it? As long as there is a market for this material, it will still be made. There will still be women who are used to make money from by having their bodies objectified. Having this stuff so accessible that people, like you, become so numb to it that they simply shrug it off as no big deal also leads to men shrugging it off as 'no big deal' when they violate a woman's sovereignty. It leads to men not even kenning what they did because they have become so numb to the sanctity of what sex actually looks like! By being a consumer of this machine, you are feeding it and are complicit in its consequences!"

I turned to walk away, and, as I did so, Jordan stood up and placed a hand on my shoulder in an attempt to stop me. I immediately wheeled around and punched him square in the face. He went down like a sack of potatoes.

I stared down at him with fury pounding in my veins. As I looked at him, I could see the man who had assaulted Annalyse when I was powerless to do anything about it. There was also a part of me who saw the version of myself that I forgave during the shadow work Shannon and I had done together. The mixture of emotions flowing through me crashed against each other with the force of two weather systems colliding together to create one super nova of a hurricane.

"What in the hell?" he mumbled as he rubbed his sore jaw.

"It is men like you who feed into the predators that rape women in alley ways," I spat.

As I turned to walk away, he swiped his legs around and kicked my own out from under me. I went down hard on the mat. It felt as though my brain had just rung inside my own head like the clapper inside a bell. Just as I was sitting up and getting my bearings about me, a sword hit the mat next to where I was sitting. I looked up to see that Jordan was armed with his own sword and was swiping it through the air.

"Ye got sum' te say? Say it," he said gesturing at the sword within my reach.

Part of me thought he must have a death wish, the other kenned his odds were pretty good since I was so out of shape.

I guess that just meant that I did not need to hold back.

I grabbed the sword and stood up, then gave it a good twisted swipe through the air.

God, I loved that sound.

Without saying another word, I pounced. Our swords clanged together like lightning hitting a mountain. It was as if Zeus himself had just hurled a bolt.

It did not take long before the wind was fought out of me. It is always surprising to me how quickly one can lose their condition in such a short time of neglect.

I stood panting while barely being able to lift my sword any longer.

"Yer outta shape," Jordan said.

In response he got a "no shit" eyebrow raise.

Not having anything more to say to him, I threw my sword down and turned to walk out.

As I was leaving, I heard him shout behind me, "I best see ye in here tomorrow!"

He would – so I could officially kick his ass.

The walk back to the house felt somewhat like a walk of shame. I did not feel like I had come out of that encounter on top, but at this point it did not matter. All I could think about was a hot shower and a healthy, wholesome meal.

Once I got back into my bedroom, I asked Aine to order some Thai food from Annalyse's favorite Thai place, Pad Noodle, then headed straight for a shower.

My hope was that by the time I finished washing, my food would be delivered.

I was right.

Just as I was toweling off, Aine informed me that the delivery woman had arrived. I slipped my robe on, and I went to go meet her at the door. As I sat to eat my food, there was something nostalgic about it. The last time I had eaten this meal had been with Annalyse before I had truly understood who she was to me. It was nice, in a way. It allowed space for me to feel more connected to her and I used it to fuel me.

As the weeks went on, I started getting back to my usual self. I was training with Jordan six days a week, keeping up with my life duties, and I had even started writing a new book.

As much as I still struggled with what was going on with Annalyse, I allowed my love for her to keep me going. I kenned she would have been heartbroken to have seen me like I was; some hollow shell of the former man that she had kenned.

No.

That was not what she was going to see when she awoke. I may not have been strong enough to protect her that night, but my mental fortitude and discipline was strong enough for this. It was strong enough for her.

It had been almost six weeks since I had last seen Shannon, and I had begun to question whether I would ever see her again. That was until one Tuesday morning when she was waiting for me in the driveway when I got home from visiting Annalyse in the hospital.

"Well, this is what I get for leaving the gates open," I said half mockingly. Half…. There was still a part of me that was frustrated with her for walking away from the work we had been doing together.

She simply gave me wry smile as she walked towards me and began following me into the house.

"What are you doing here?" I asked as politely as I could manage.

"Aine contacted me," she said very matter of factly.

"Oh?" I replied while taking a mental note to see about Aine's programing, but then let that thought go quickly, as I kenned I would be hopeless at trying to sort through any of her programs. "And why would she have done such a thing?"

"Because I asked her to."

"I do not ken what you are on about, Shannon," I responded as I sat down on one of the bar stools at the kitchen counter.

I was not happy to see her.

I found it very annoying, in fact, that she would show up now after all these weeks – after I had finally gotten myself back on track.

Pulling up a chair next to me, she filled me in.

"I asked Aine to let me know when you finally got your shit back together. She contacted me last night to let me know you had had a consecutive twenty-one days of being back to your normal state of mental health, which she deemed was sufficient... so here I am."

"Ah," I said with a dramatic head nod as if to express my faux gratitude for her prodigal return. "And what does that mean for me?"

She gave me a penetrating look that implied that I was a complete numpty before responding.

"That it's time to get back to work."

CHAPTER 12

It felt so good to rest.

Michael was the most amazing man and partner. I understood why having dreamt I had been separated from him would have caused me so much pain. He was perfect. Tending to my every need, honoring me, and treating me like a queen.

I didn't quite understand why I felt the need to rest so much, as my life was pretty much picture perfect, but alas, I did. Regardless of the perfection, I still felt so tired. Not in the sense of needing sleep, but just needing rest. It was like my spirit was tired, not so much my body. I felt so fortunate to have such a loving husband, that though laird of the castle, and there were plenty of others who could help tend to me, he made sure to be the one to do so.

"How are you today, my darling?" he asked as he helped adjust the pillows behind my back.

The sun had been up for hours, but I was still resting in bed. It felt kind of silly having this large, strong man tending to me in such a way when I was perfectly well, but yet it felt so right. Like this was why I was here. To be loved and adored and taken care of.

I took a deep sigh of contentment and gave Michael a sweet smile and said, "Anything with you is absolutely perfect."

He kissed me on the nose and smiled back at me in response.

"I could not agree more, my beloved. Would you like me to read to you again, my dear?" he asked.

"That would be lovely," I said smiling.

I loved the books he read to me. It seemed as if that was what we spent most of our time doing. He told me that the books were very special ones he had gotten from a wise woman that he met one day when he was hunting in the woods. She had told him that the fairies had written them for me, and they were filled with their wisdom. Knowing how drawn I was to the fairies in the woods, he brought them back home to me and we kept them our little secret.

Michael sat down in the chair next to the bed and picked up the book that had been placed on the nightstand from the last time he had read it to me. I sat back and closed my eyes as he began.

None of it ever made any sense to my ears. It was as if he were speaking a different language of some sort, but it didn't matter. I knew what it meant. I let the words wash over me like light codes. The vibrations of the words felt amazing. It was as though they had their own energy and as he spoke them over me, I could feel my strength returning to me and growing within me.

Not that I was in any hurry for this doting to end.

It felt like I was basking in heaven. A paradise of bliss and ecstasy all wrapped into a very strong and handsome man. Spending time with the love of my eternal soul, while being bathed in the warm, sweet energy of the beautiful stories he read to me, was a type of bliss that I never could have imagined for myself.

I laid back and listened, allowing the words leave his lips and wash over me like a warm current guiding me off to where I was meant to be.

As Michael read, I felt myself drift away on his words.

I found myself walking through the woods where, directly in front of me, there was a large clearing. In the clearing was a beautiful, crystal clear lake that was being fed by a waterfall. I found it very interesting that, though the waterfall rained down into the lake, the surface of the water was rather calm and placid.

I walked towards it to place my hand on the surface. I could feel the water, but it wasn't wet. It was almost as if it were made of some type of matter that no one had discovered before. The substance felt like a combination of liquid and air. The temperature was also exactly that of my skin, as I felt no temperature difference at all between the substance and my skin.

It felt amazing.

All I could think was how much I would love to swim in this lake. I looked around trying to see if anyone else was around, and, after I was satisfied with the notion that I was alone here, I slipped off my white shift, and leaving it behind me on the cool grass, I slowly walked my way into the lake.

I let out an audible sigh of pleasure as the substance wrapped itself around every inch of my body that it came into contact with. The deeper I went, the better it felt. As the pool got deeper I pushed myself forward with my feet across the surface of the lake and breast stroked my way out into the more open water. I felt so light and free. I couldn't help but let out a joyful laugh. I felt so playful in this sweet pool of nectar.

Finally, I got brave and decided to put my face under the surface, and, to my wonder, I could see perfectly clearly and also had no need to hold my breath. Excitement thrilling through me, I dived under the surface and began to explore. The pool was filled with beautiful crystals of all shapes, sizes, and colors. They emitted a glow that allowed me to see as I swam through the miraculous substance.

Everything was so magnificent.

After enjoying frolicking in the water like a mermaid for some time, I came up to the surface with the thought of exploring the waterfall and the other beautiful scenery in this magical space, and was very surprised by what I saw when my head broke the surface of the water.

There was a man crouched down at the edge of the water examining my under garment. He appeared to be well built and tall with light hair and blue eyes. He wore all white.

I was amazed to realize that I felt no fear at seeing this man here in this space. He seemed familiar in a way. He dropped my dress and stood up once he saw my head hovering on the surface of the substance I had been swimming in. I knew the lake was perfectly clear so he could most likely see my naked body as I treaded in place, but I didn't care. I simply stared at him as he looked at me, his eyes never moving from my face.

"Is this yours?" I asked as I looked around. I was quite a ways away from him, but he heard me perfectly fine.

"No, lass, it is yours," he said.

"I've never been here before nor have I seen this space before. Where did it come from?"

"I built it for you, in hopes that it would help you heal," he replied.

I found this to be a very odd statement.

"Am I ill?" I asked as I slowly made my way back to the shore.

"No. Your body is in good health," he told me.

"Then what is it that needs healing? What am I healing from?" I felt bad asking so many questions, but he seemed to have answers, and I wanted them.

"You *are* healing."

That wasn't much of a clear answer, but it seemed satisfactory enough. I climbed out of the pool and *walked over to him, picked up my shift and put it on. I could tell he was trying to be respectful, but I felt no need for him to act like it was shameful to want to look at my body. It was beautiful. Why wouldn't he want to look at it?*

"If this space is for me, why are you here?" I said examining his features.

"I do not ken, lass. I guess I got lucky."

I just smiled at him and let out a small chuckle.

"May I show you something?" he asked as he stretched out his hand.

I did not take it, but instead nodded. He dropped his hand, attempting to mask the sting he felt from the rejection. All I could think was "Really? You're upset about me not wanting to take your hand? You got to see me naked. You're welcome."

We walked a ways into the forest until we entered another clearing. This one was much smaller than the one we had just left. It looked like a perfect circle with small, flat, round stones laid around the edge. As I walked through the space, I noted that there were twelve and each stone had a drawing on it of a moon phase.

"What is this space for?" I asked, as I turned around to look at the man who had led me here.

When I turned around though, I was surprised to see a woman standing with him. She appeared to be middle aged with a curvy figure. Her hair was the color of flames and she had blue eyes. She looked at me with kindness and curiosity.

It was her who answered my question. "This is a portal that was created so that we could come to you."

I was astounded by this answer.

"Why would you do such a thing?" I asked utterly perplexed.

They looked at each other as if trying to decide how to answer so I added, "Why would you want to visit me in my dreams?"

They looked at each other again as if surprised by the information that I just shared.

"So, lass, you are telling us that right now you are dreaming?" the man asked.

"Yes," I laughed. "Of course! How else could I breathe under a water-like substance that didn't feel wet to swim in, or why I wouldn't care that you saw me naked getting out of the pool? This isn't real. It's just a dream."

They looked at each other as if unsure of what they were supposed to do with this information.

"Why are you here?" I asked.

It was the man who answered. "We thought you might be lost, and we were trying to help you find your way back."

"Oh," I said feeling perplexed. "I don't think I am lost at all. I just have to wake up."

"Aye, lass. We were hoping to help you wake up," he said.

"Why?"

"Because you have work to do," he responded slowly, as if being very picky about the words he used before he let them slip between his lips.

"Oh… no. I think you have me confused with someone else. I have been too tired to work. I have been resting as my husband takes care of me."

The man looked as if he wanted to say something more, as if my words had hurt him in some way, but the woman placed her hand on his arm to stop him and looked him deliberately in the eyes. She then turned to me and said, "If you need rest. You should rest." Then turning her attention back to the man she said, "We should go."

He looked as if he were about to panic for a minute. I stepped back from him as his energy intensified towards me. I could feel it pushing against me like heat radiating off a fire. I guess something about my reaction to his intensity affected him in some way because his shoulders slumped slightly, in defeat, and he looked at the woman and said, "Aye," in barely a whisper.

I decided that was my cue to make my way back to my lake, so I began walking in the direction we had entered the clearing in. I hesitated for a moment, then turned around to address the man that was staring at me as if he were in agony. "Thank you for making this space for me. It is absolutely beautiful. I'm sorry, I cannot give you what you want."

I then turned back around and made my way back to my lake.

As I walked through the forest, I realized that I had been moving in a different direction than the one we had come. It didn't worry me as I felt completely safe here and knew that I would find where I needed to go.

Sure enough, ahead I could see a lantern hanging next to what looked like a door that was carved into a very large tree. There we stepping stones that lead the way to the door and I followed them. The door was arched and looked very old. The metal fixtures on it were rusted and had clearly seen many years.

I looked up at the lantern that hung to the left of the door and noticed there was an inscription just beneath it. It appeared to me in a foreign language that looked as if it wasn't even human. Even though it was not a tongue that I recognized, I still knew what it said.

COME THE MAGIC OF THE LIGHT

THE DARKNESS FADES AWAY

WITHIN THE WOUND THE MAGIC GROWS

WITHOUT THE LIGHT, THERE IT WILL STAY

I spoke it aloud as I read it, and, as if it was a secret phrase to unlock the door on the tree, the door moved inward and permitted me passage inside.

I hesitated for a moment, but, then, reminding myself that this was just a dream, I pushed the door further open and stepped inside.

What I found was not what I expected. The space was large and warm, filled with candles and books.

Books everywhere.

As I made my way completely inside, I was suddenly rushed upon by several delightfully cheerful children. Or at least I thought they were children.

When I took a step back from them, I realized they were actually full-grown, having characteristics and features like that of a fully matured adult, but looking oddly proportioned. Their eyes were all very large and innocent looking, while their nose and mouth were very small. Their skin had a pearlescent sheen to it that made them appear to slightly glow in the warm candlelight, and their ears were large and pointed at the ends.

These were fairies.

And they were so excited to see me.

"She's here!" one chirped with his high-pitched voice.

"We knew you would come!" said another as she grabbed my hand and held it with gleeful adoration.

The others simply beamed up at me, while I looked around at their happy, rosy faces.

"I'm sorry," I said. "Have you been expecting me?"

They looked around in confusion about how to answer this question until the female holding my hand spoke first.

"Why yes, miss. We have something for you!"

The group of five fairies scrambled away as quickly as they had come to me and ran up a flight up stairs to my left. I couldn't help but giggle at their excitement. They truly reminded me of little *children at Christmas time. I watched them through the balcony railing from down below as they scampered and searched for what they were seeking.*

"Here it is!" squeaked another of the male fairies as he grabbed a large, ancient looking book and raised it over his head.

Careful not to drop it, he and his companions made their way slowly back down the staircase to place the book on a nearby table.

I looked at them as I made my way over to the table to meet them. Their faces were eager and alight with hope and joy.

I smiled down on them, and they all beamed back up at me.

"Here, miss! Here!" one of the female fairies told me. "Here it is! For you! We have kept it safe and well protected for you like you told us."

Her words took me by surprise.

"Like I told you?" I asked confused. "Have I been here before?"

They again looked at each other as if unsure how to respond.

"It's okay," I said. "It would help me a lot of you would tell me."

Finally, the female fairy, who had most recently spoken to me, answered me.

"Why yes, mistress Theia. You visited with us many moon cycles ago and left this book of ancient knowledge, telling us that, if you were ever to return, we must give it to you and never share it with any others."

"Theia? Did you say Theia?"

I felt as though that name sounded familiar, but I couldn't recall ever hearing it before. It was as if I could barely brush up against the edge of the memory, but when I grasped for it, it would turn to smoke.

"Yes, mistress. 'Tis how you introduced yourself to us."

She looked around at the other fairies for support and they all nodded in unison.

"But you must be mistaken. My name isn't Theia. It's...."

Well, that was odd. I couldn't seem to remember my own name.

I stood there for a few moments simply staring at the fairies as they watched me with hopefulness.

"Please look miss!" said the female again. "It is what you asked us to keep for you. You said it was

very important that it stay safe and that you would be back for it when you needed it. We did as you asked of us mistress. It is here! For you."

She gently shoved me in my side to force my attention onto the book.

The book was very large and brown with intricate designs on the front. There were also symbols on the front. I knew immediately that they were an activation code written in Light Language, but how I knew this was again like grasping at the smoky memory of the name Theia. It was right there, but just out of reach.

As I laid my hands upon the book and moved my fingertips across the front cover, both the cover and the tips of my fingers began to glow with a soft, golden light.

I quickly moved my hands and jerked them away from the surface of the book. The fairies watched me intently.

The book hadn't hurt me, I was simply startled by what had happened.

Summoning my courage, I reached out for the book again.

I watched the golden light grow and noticed how the symbols seemed to pulsate with the glowing, gold light. Using my pointer finger, I traced one of the symbols and without warning I had a rush of memories flood into my brain.

I closed my eyes and could feel them flickering behind my eyelids as if I were dreaming, as flash after flash of images chased each other across my mind. The images were too fast for me to grasp any details from any of them.

Once they stopped, I took my hand away from the book and stared at my hand.

I noticed that my fingernails looked different. They were long and pointed and very light in color. They also seemed to have some of the pearlescence to them that matched the fairies' skin.

I looked up at the fairies and they all beamed at me in delight before gently bowing their heads.

"Forgive me," I said. "But why are you bowing?"

They again looked amongst each other before the female spoke again.

"Because mistress, we are here to serve you as part of your angelic team for support and guidance on your soul's mission."

My soul's mission? How could my soul be on a mission when I was the most happy and content woman in the world? I felt like I was living my

*mission, by being with Michael. He was all I have
ever wanted.*

"I don't understand," I said, looking over at her.

*"'Tis all in the book mistress," she replied gesturing
back to the book.*

"Oh," I said as I began to open the book. "I see."

*"NO MISS!" she squealed as she placed her hand on
top of the book cover, preventing me from opening
it. "Not here. You must open it when you are
ready."*

I looked at her in surprise and confusion.

"'Tis what you told us miss."

*I slowly moved my hands back away from the book
and said, "Okay then, but how will I know when I
am ready?"*

"Because you will find the book again."

*This answer didn't make any sense to me because I
had just found it. Here and now.*

She then added, "Goodbye, mistress!"

I suddenly opened my eyes to see Michael sitting
beside me, with the book he had been reading me
still in hand.

CHAPTER 13

Henry

All I could do was cry, and I hated it.

I resented the warmth as it ran down my face, carving its way through the stubble in my beard. Each warm stream, a reminder of my failure.

I had done it.

I had been so close.

I had found her.

We did it!

Yet here I still was. Alone. Without her.

It was as if she did not even recognize me or ken who I was. It was as if Michael had become the reality and I the illusion.

After sending Shannon home, I had a complete fit of hysterics. I kenned it was coming, and I did not want her to see me express myself in this way for fear that she would think I had hopped back on the train to Henry Hell and would refuse to help me anymore.

I had trusted her, and she helped me get to Annalyse, but instead of helping me fight for her she pulled me out of the hypnotic trance. It was as if every time I felt like I made any progress forward it was negated by a setback. Sometimes unforeseen and others deliberate, it seemed.

"Come on Henry, pull yourself together," I said aloud. "You did it! You reached her. That is something."

A voice responded to me and it startled me, I looked up to see Aine's screen flashing as she responded to what I had just said.

"Yes, sir, and now you know you found her through a subconscious back door."

I was confused by this statement.

"What do you mean, Aine?"

"She was 'dreaming' when you were able to make contact, so it sounds like she is going in and out of various stages of consciousness. If you can track her brainwaves, you will know when she is dreaming again and know when it is best to go in again."

Well, shit.

"Aine, I would say you're a genius but as you are a machine I do not ken if it would be as much of a compliment as you deserve."

She flashed her screen pale pink as if to mimic blushing and said, "Thank you, sir."

After this revelation, brought to being thanks to Aine, I decided to go to the hospital earlier than I had originally planned.

Once I got there, I asked for Annie and was grateful to learn that she had been the nurse on shift since this morning, right after I had left, and it turned out that her shift was nearing its end, so I had arrived just in time to speak with her.

Annie entered the room as I was pulling the chair in the room over closer to Annalyse's bedside.

"Henry?" I heard in a kind tone from behind me.

I looked up to see the nurse standing there looking at me curiously.

"You were asking to see me?" she continued.

"Aye, lass. I was," I told her as I turned to face her. Call me old fashioned, but I felt that I should stay standing while addressing a woman.

"Am I correct in understanding that Annalyse's brain waves are being monitored regularly?"

Annie looked at me quizzically before responding with, "Why yes, of course. All comatose patients have their brain waves monitored."

I simply nodded in response, as I tried to figure out how to word my next question.

As she watched me, I could feel sweat starting to form on the back of my neck. How could I possibly explain why I was inquiring about her brainwaves?

Presumably, Annie sensed my nerves and had the mercy to rescue me from my soon-to-be panic and responded with the answer to the question she thought I wanted to ask.

"I'm sorry, Henry. Nothing has changed."

Her tone was compassionate and kind, but her words were not what I was seeking.

"Oh. Aye, lass. I ken. I ken you would notify me if anything did."

It was obvious that Annie was feeling confused again as she asked, "Then... what is it that you were hoping to know?"

It was in this moment where I decided that the truth was the best course of action, so I asked.

"Well, to be honest, lass, I was actually wondering if Annalyse has been dreaming?"

This surprised her.

"Oh, well I suppose so. When someone sleeps, their brain waves change and one would be able to decipher if that individual were in a dream state or not." Walking over to the monitor she added, "Why do you ask?"

As she began looking at the readings from the monitor, I again decided that sticking to the truth was the best idea. Or as close to the truth as I could be without Annie thinking I was mental.

"I had a dream about her, and this dream made me wonder about the possibility of her having dreams as well."

Annie looked up from the readings to give me another compassionate smile and said, "That's so sweet."

I gave a small nod and smile back in response just before she added, "And look." She pointed at a section of the readings, "This was probably the last time she dreamed," she said as she looked up at me with a full smile before adding, "Maybe you dreamed together."

I kenned her statement was meant to be supportive and kind, as she most likely would not have believed me if I said, "Aye! Sure did!" So, instead, I just said, "Aye. Maybe," while matching her smile.

"Was that all?" Annie asked.

"Aye, lass. That is all."

"Okay, then," she said as she turned to leave the room. "I'm off my shift now. Dillon is on the next shift in case you need anything from him."

I watched Annie walk out the door and then began examining Annalyse's readouts. I could see the pattern where her readings showed the change in peaks on the paper. I examined the timestamps more closely to see that the last time the peaks showed dream state it was indeed around the same time that Shannon and I had gone through the portal that she had created.

"What are you doing?"

I jumped at the sound of the familiar voice behind me.

"I'm sorry," Morgan said. "I didn't mean to startle you."

I laughed. God, I was jumpy. It was not like I was doing something sinister by reading a brainwave report.

"I was just looking at Annalyse's readings to see if anything looked different."

"And?" Morgan inquired.

"Afraid not. Though I did learn that she has been dreaming."

"Oh really? Well, that's a good sign, right?"

"Aye. I would say so."

Morgan hovered for a moment and then said, "I hadn't expected to see you here, but since you are, I can go…"

Her words trailed off as she made a movement towards the door.

"No. Please do not leave," I said as a bold idea came to mind.

"I actually could use your help with something, if you do not mind?"

Morgan looked at me with a raised brow, clearly uncertain if she wanted to help me, before asking, "And what is it that you want my help with?"

"It is about Annalyse."

Morgan's body language immediately softened.

"I'm listening."

I took a deep breath and asked, "Did you plan to stay with her for a while today?"

There came that suspicion again.

"Yes. I had planned that. Why?"

"I was wondering if you would be willing to let me ken when her brain patterns change again, to look like this." I showed her the section of the reading that Annie had shown me.

Morgan peered over the paper that was in my hands and then looked up at me with confusion.

"Why?"

"I would not ken how to explain," I told her.

"Look, Henry. I think it's obvious by now that I love Annalyse. She is my family. I want to help. There is clearly something strange going on here." She waved her hands between Annalyse and me. "I've seen you and that Shannon woman having whispered conversations and you just popped up out of nowhere. I get it. Annalyse has always been a private person, and I suppose this is your way of honoring that, but I feel like the kid who is being

238

left out at the lunch table. I'm here too. Showing up, helping how I can, but I'm still being left out of the loop. This has been hell for me too, Henry. Feeling like I am being left out of some big secret isn't helping."

I had kenned that this was a challenging time for Morgan, as well as myself, but I had not thought about how much I had been isolating her, especially when she had extended me so much kindness.

"You are right Morgan, and I apologize." I took a deep breath before continuing. "Shannon is a type of spiritual guru. To be honest, I do not ken if she has an actual title in her work, but she has been helping me try to reconnect to Annalyse on a spirit level as Annalyse and I are a type of soulmate and are very bonded in a spiritual way."

Morgan stood in front of me for a few minutes, nodding her head and pursing her lips, before she shrugged.

"Okay."

She shrugged again as she worked to process what I had just told her. I waited silently as I held space for her.

"Okay," she repeated. "So, what does the reading," she pointed at the paper I was still holding in my hand, "have to do with anything?"

Since she was asking for honesty, I decided to give it to her.

"Earlier today I connected with Annalyse through a sort of dream state. I found out that she had also been dreaming at the same time. I wanted to try to connect with her again when she is dreaming."

There, I said it.

I stood frozen to the spot waiting for her to tell me how ridiculous I was and that I was dangerous and deranged and should not be allowed near her best friend, but Morgan surprised me.

"You saw her?" She asked. "You spoke with her?"

To my astonishment, I could see tears forming in her waterlines.

"Aye. I did."

Morgan walked around me to sit down in the chair that I had pulled over next to Annalyse's bed and then looked up at me with misty eyes.

"What did she say?"

This was not what I was expecting, so I had to switch my mental gears quickly to pivot with the direction of the conversation.

"She was confused," I began slowly. "It was as if she did not ken who I was. She thought she was just dreaming, and I was simply a visitor that had been concocted from her imagination."

Morgan surprising me still, reached up to gently touch my arm and said, "Oh, Henry. I'm so sorry."

I looked down at her grieving face and said, "Aye, me too."

After moving her hand from my arm to rest it on Annalyse's hand, Morgan looked back up at me and said, "Go home and lay down. I will text you as soon as I see her readings change."

"Thank you, Morgan."

As I was driving home, the sun was just beginning to set. It painted the sky with oranges, pinks, and purples. It was stunning. All I could think was how beautiful Annalyse would look as the bright orange light shone across her pale skin and red hair. She would be glorious.

On my way home, Shannon called me to check in – which made me wonder if Aine was still spying for her.

"Aye?" I said, as I pushed the button on my steering wheel to answer the phone.

"Where are you?" she asked.

Great, now she wanted me to account to her my outings.

"I went by the hospital to check in on Annalyse. Aine helped me fill in some gaps in our theories and I wanted to verify what she had said."

"Oh really?"

I could tell she was interested that we might have a new development.

"Aye, really."

"And what did you figure out?"

I took a deep breath before filling her in. It felt nice for a change to ken more than she did.

"Aine had concluded that Annalyse was easier to access when in a dream state because her mind was more relaxed and open to suggestions. Less pushback."

"Right," she said, slightly impatiently. "But why would you need to go to the hospital to confirm this?"

"Because Aine had also said that they were most likely keeping track of her brainwaves, and, in those reports, there should be a record of when she was in dream state. She was right. Also, Annalyse was, in fact in a dream state earlier today when we made contact. Morgan is there now to keep an eye on her readings to let me know when to try to make contact again."

"Oh?" she asked, slightly surprised. "Did you finally let Morgan in on your and Annalyse's true connection?"

"Not entirely, no. I simply told her that we had a very deep, spiritual bond and that I had made contact with Annalyse in a dream and I wanted to try again. I supposed she did not see any harm in me trying again."

"Well, I agree with her on that. I'm on my way over."

And with that, she hung up.

Christ.

I truly appreciated Shannon's help, and still did not quite understand why or how she was so invested in this, but the constant showing up unannounced and inviting herself over was getting to me.

By the time I had pulled into my garage, I could see Shannon coming to a park in the driveway.

I reluctantly waved her in behind me as I made my way into the house through the garage entrance.

"Have you heard anything from Morgan?" Shannon asked as we made our way down the hallway into the kitchen.

"No, not yet."

I went to the refrigerator to grab a bottle of sparkling water.

"Want some?" I offered.

"Sure."

Just as I handed her the bottle, I heard my phone vibrate on the counter.

I almost spilled my own water down the front of myself when I heard it buzz like an angry bubble bee that was trapped inside a jar.

Shannon and I looked at each other in anticipation.

I slowly picked up my phone to check the message and my body relaxed.

"It is just Jordan. He was giving me a verbal skelping for not showing up for our training session today." Placing my phone back down on the counter I added, "I had totally forgotten about it because I had gotten so distracted by the revelation Aine had uncovered."

"That's understandable, Henry. Just don't get too lost in the circumstances that you lose yourself again."

I gave her a stern look. I was not in the mood for a lecture.

"I ken what you mean. Today was a one-off. I am allowed to have off days still, am I not?"

Shannon put her hands up in surrender as she responded.

"Okay, okay. I'm just trying to help."

"I ken you are, and I am grateful for it, but sometimes it can be a bit overbearing for my taste. I cannot seem to comprehend why you are so eager to help. Even when I thought you were no longer willing to help, it turns out you were just having Aine spy on me for you? It has gotten to be pretty intense."

Shannon walked over to the living room and sat down in one of the chairs looking slightly defeated.

"Here's the thing, Henry. I haven't been in full disclosure with you."

All I wanted to say was "No shit," but my manners would not allow me to. So, instead I kept my mouth shut and went to sit with her in the living room.

"I know you have been wondering why I have been so attached to this situation and so willing to drop everything to help you," she said while looking down at her clasped hands in her lap.

I felt my heart begin to beat faster with fear. With these words, my mind immediately went to the thought that she was going to confess feelings for me that I did not return. Do not get me wrong, Shannon was wonderful, but she was not Annalyse.

I sat still and quiet, as my stomach knotted in anticipation for her continued explanation.

Shannon took a deep breath, looked up at me, and said, "Annalyse is my sister."

Nothing. Nothing could have prepared me for this information.

This new revelation hit me like I had just been pushed into a pool of ice water. I stared at Shannon, slack jawed in response.

"She was also once my daughter, a friend, a lover, and many other things before. We have had many lifetimes together. I remember you from the last incarnation you two spent together. Do you remember me? I worked as a maid in your house. My name then was Mary."

I rubbed my stubbled jaw, then ran my hand through my hair as I worked to process what she was telling me.

"So, what you are telling me, Shannon, is that you are Annalyse's actual sister in this lifetime and have been close to her in many lifetimes preceding this one?"

"Yes."

"Alright," I began as I stood up to pace around. Moving helped the thoughts to flow. "I can understand the past life connections, but it is you being her sister that I do not ken how is possible."

She nodded.

"That's understandable; Annalyse and I were both orphans."

"She never mentioned that too me," I said, feeling a pain of loss tug at my insides. There was so much I did not ken about Annalyse that I wanted to ken. I wanted to ken everything.

"It's very possible that she never mentioned it because she most likely doesn't know. When our parents died, we had no other family, so we went into the foster care system. I was twelve and she was just a few months old, and, as babies were easier to adopt out, they separated us. I spent the remainder of my childhood in the system until I turned eighteen. Though I have never made contact, I have still kept an eye on her all these years."

My whole body was covered with chill bumps from the top of my head down to my feet. How sad and tragic for both of these women. Though Annalyse may have never kenned about this, I kenned there had to be a part of her that felt that loss and separation. Thinking about all the pain that she has been through brought moisture into my eyes.

I squatted down in front of Shannon and took her clenched hands in mine.

"Thank you for trusting me enough to share this information with me. We will get her back."

And just in that same moment we could hear my phone buzzing again on the counter. I stood up, walked into the kitchen, and picked it up to see a message from Morgan. Filled with as much anticipation as I was, Shannon had walked over to join me and peered over my shoulder as I open the message.

There were three words on the screen: Go get her.

CHAPTER 14

When I had woken up, I noticed that Michael had stopped reading out loud and was sitting in the chair next to the bed reading to himself.

"How do you feel, beloved?" he asked, after realizing I was watching him.

I took a deep breath and gave my body a cognitive examination from head to toe before responding.

"Better," I said, as I let the air out of my lungs.

A huge smile spread across his face that I couldn't help but match.

"I'm so glad. Did you have any dreams?"

"I did. I dreamt of a beautiful lake in the middle of a lush forest. The lake was crystal clear and was filled with a substance unlike any I've experienced in the waking world. I could breathe in it as I swam. It was so much fun!"

He smiled as he watched me tell him about my experience swimming in the magical lake.

"Then once I was done swimming, I came to the surface and saw a man crouched down next to my shift. He showed me what he described as a portal where a female companion of his was waiting. I felt like he wanted me to go with him."

Michael looked slightly alarmed by this part of the story.

"And did you want to go with him?" he asked as he sat the book on the table to give our conversation his full attention.

"No. No, I did not," I said firmly as a looked at him with determination. "Besides, why would it matter? It was just a dream anyways."

After making what I thought was an obvious statement, his posture relaxed as he sat back in his chair.

"Aye, it was only a dream."

I smiled at him and raised my eyebrow in a teasing sort of way.

"Is there more, my beloved?" he asked quizzically.

"As a matter of fact, there is. The lake and the man with his friend showing me the portal was just the beginning of what I dreamed – and if you can believe it, the dream got even stranger," I continued.

"Oh?" he asked with apt interest.

"Yep!" I responded as I sat up more on the bed to get a better look at him.

"I dreamed that I came across a secret fairy shop that was full of old books! And it was hidden inside a tree!"

"A magical fairy book shop in a tree? Well, lass, that does sound much better than an odd man wanting you to go through a portal with him and his companion."

I laughed.

"Yes, it was. The fairies were so happy and excited to see me. They called me by a name that of course I can't remember now, and gave me a very old book that made my fingers glow when I touched it."

Michael smiled as I told him all about how happy and excited the fairies were and how it felt to touch the book and to see my fingers glow.

"Well, lass, it sounds like your kind of shop," he said, then kissed me on the forehead before adding, "I am glad your dream ended on a light note."

Michael then stood up and walked around to the other side of the bed and laid down next to me on his side, propped up on his left elbow. Using his right hand, he gently drew his fingers across my face, tracing my jawline.

"Thank you for sharing your adventures with me," he added.

As I stared into his eyes, I could see an endless ocean of love that I craved to float away on. I rolled my body over to face his and mirrored his motions. I loved tracing the lines of his face. He had mild dimple in his chin that drew attention to his strong jawline. His lips were soft as my fingers traced them. I loved how full his lips were and that his top lip was slightly off balance like mine. It gave way for his perfect, signature, half smile.

Continuing to allow his features to talk to me through my fingertips, I traced down his broad nose, that also had a minute dimple at the end that complimented the one on his chin. Something about these little details drew me in so strongly. I also loved tracing his prominent cheek bones, as I felt the stubble of his hairs beneath my sensitive fingertips. His brow wrinkled a little as he studied me studying him. I smiled at the sight and traced the lines on his forehead, sweeping aside a few pieces of dark hair.

"What is it, beloved?" he asked in a whisper.

"You," I said with a faint smile as I continued to trace his features. "You are perfect. My ideal man. The perfect expression of the masculine in physical form. If I could have placed an order with God himself to create the exact man that I wanted, you would be what was delivered."

I let out a contented sigh, then added, "I want to drink you in."

"Aye, lass. As do I...." he said as his own tracing hand trailed down my neck to find my collarbone. It then lightly danced across the sensitive skin between my collarbones before his finger slowly made its way down to the tie on my night dress. He watched my face the entire time his finger glided across my skin, watching my reaction. I could tell he was making sure that the touching was something I wanted and was enjoying.

It was.

I was.

To cue him into that fact, I slid my body closer to his and gently touched the tip of his nose with my own. It was clear that he received my signal, as he closed his eyes, while placing his forehead on mine, and let out a gentle sigh. His lips held a faint smile as he reveled in the anticipation of what was about to happen.

To my surprise, he slowly pulled away, got up, and made his way back over to the chair in which had had recently vacated not moments before.

After sitting down, he looked at me with a fire burning in his eyes.

"Come here, my darling" he told me.

As I stood up to come closer to him, he gently aided me in removing my night gown. He then turned my body so that I was facing away from him and placing his hands on the bare skin on my waist helped me onto his lap. Slowly, his hands began to trail up the front of my body until they reached the base of my breasts. Lifting his hands off my skin ever so slightly, he brough them overtop of my breasts, holding them, hovering just over my sensitive skin.

I could feel the heat of his palms reaching for the heat that was building up inside myself. Even without contact, I could feel his energy pouring into my breasts. It was as if I were drawing his energy into myself. I allowed myself to soak up his energy as my head fell back onto his shoulder and I let out a moan of pleasure.

As my head rested on his shoulder, he drew his nose up the side of my neck and face, taking in my scent. Then, ever so gently, he began kissing the sensitive skin at the back of my jaw just beneath my ear. My breath quaked as it entered my body, causing my chest to expand, pushing itself closer into his awaiting hands, but they did not make contact. Instead, I felt stimulation in a different part of my body. Michael had opened his legs, allowing mine to rest on either side of them, then slowly rocking his hips back and forth, forced my own to move in unison. As my sensitive areas gained friction on his leg I let out another moan of pleasure.

"Yes...." Michael whispered in my ear as he finally brought his hands into contact with my breasts, causing me to moan again.

As I panted in anticipation, he slid his left hand up my chest to hold my body closer to his, then slowly moved his right hand down my abdomen until it stopped in between by legs.

With the contact of his hand my back arched and he held me firmly to him body.

I then turned my head to look him in his beautiful blue eyes and said, "I want you."

He looked over every inch of pleasure on my face before responding, "I am yours."

Then he kissed me. It was deep and passionate, yet soft.

After a few moments in our fervent kiss, Michael moved his hands to my sides and helped me move from his lap back onto the bed. Then he climbed on top of my quivering body, holding his weight off me so I could just barely feel the pressure of his form against mine.

His hand held the side of my face hungrily, though with an added gentleness. I could feel his passion along with his restraint. He was stronger than I was both physically and with his restraint. Unlike him, I made no effort to hold back my desire for him.

Utilizing his imbalanced and restrained position, I thrust my body to the side, forcing him off me and onto his back next to me. I then rolled up on top of him, one leg on either side of his large, strong body and rolled my hips over the mound I was straddling. I gave a moan of pleasure at the contact of my need.

His teasing had left my body craving for more, and it wanted everything and all of him.

I could tell that Michael had been taken off guard by my passion and aggression. A smile broke across his face, and his hands made their way to the roots of my hair, at the base of my skull, where they carefully intertwined.

Using the leverage, Michael gently pulled my hair causing my head to tilt backwards, exposing my throat.

I felt his warm tongue trail its way up my exposed throat until it met the sensitive skin just beneath my ear and behind my jaw line again. There, he placed a kiss before letting his warm breath escape his lips. My body shook with want, as the warmth of his breath collided with my skin.

Releasing my hair, his hands slid down to my shoulders and down my arms. This slight movement created a small breeze that swept its way across my exposed chest. I could feel my nipples reacting to the cool air.

Michael noticed them too. His hands each grasped one of my breasts, filling each hand. Using his thumbs, he massaged my nipples, causing me to rock my hips back and forth more fervently on top of him. He dropped his head back on his pillow, closed his eyes, and let out a moan that sent shivers down my spine.

Grabbing my hips, he lifted me off him so that he could loose his want for me from his pants. I then pulled down his pants and helped him remove them.

There stood his longing for me.

It was beautiful.

I loved how a whole man looked.

Grasping him with one hand, I then trailed my tongue up from the base of him until reaching the tip before wrapping my lips around him.

He moaned as his hips rolled slightly in welcome of the warmth and wetness of my mouth.

Using my hand with my mouth I moved up and down, reveling in the sounds of his moans until he stopped me and said, "Now darling, I can't have all the fun." He then patted on his hips and said, "Come, let's have a seat, aye?" with a wicked little single eyebrow raise.

I smiled in response, as I crawled up his body and then sat down upon him.

Oh god, there it was.

That deep connection I craved. As our bodies became one, our souls danced together in joy. We may have been rubbing together physically, but it was our souls that were connecting.

I leaned down to kiss him, as his hands grasped my bottom. Just then, I could feel one of his fingers make contact with the sensitive area there, and he lightly massaged me as I rocked back and forth on him. The extra sensory stimulation pushed me over the edge.

Feeling my back arch in anticipation to my climax, Michael looked me deeply in the eyes and said, "Let me in."

I found this to be a slightly odd thing to say as he clearly was "in," but the thought came and went quickly in the intensity of the moment.

I stared into his eyes as I climaxed, allowing him to witness the magic that was transpiring in my soul.

Just as he felt me convulsing around him, he also released himself. The energetic exchange between the two of us lit my soul on fire. I let my head rock back and looked up at the ceiling.

In that moment, I may as well have been god.

CHAPTER 15
Henry

I sat straight up and looked down at my crotch as I realized I had just ejaculated all over myself.

You have got to be fucking kidding me!

I looked over at Shannon unsure how to react.

"So...." She said casually, obviously trying to hide her smile. "I take it, you made some level of contact?"

Oh my God.

So, obviously she kenned about my... situation.

"Aye. If you will excuse me for a few minutes?" I said, gesturing towards the door with my head.

"Of course," she replied with a coy smile. "I will wait out in the kitchen while you... freshen up."

She then stood up and made her way out the door, shutting it firmly after exiting my room.

My mind was reeling.

Annalyse was having sex with Michael? What?! And not just sex, but mind blowing, explosive, soul shattering sex. How could my mind possibly be capable of processing something like this? My past life lover who I just reconnected with in this lifetime through my ex-wife's body, is now in a coma having an affair with the past life version of myself?

Again, what the fuck?

This was some next level relationship drama that I was nowhere near equipped for. I highly doubted that even the most highly trained couple's therapist in the world would have any applicable skill level for this situation.

I grabbed a pair of pants off the top of the "in between clean and dirty" chair pile on my way into the bathroom. Once in front of the mirror, I placed my hands on the counter to give myself a little extra balance before looking myself square in the eyes, and said, "We will get her back."

Unbuckling my belt and unbuttoning my pants I pushed them off along with my boxer briefs and tossed them over into the laundry hamper. I could smell myself too strongly still, on my skin, so I decided to hop in the shower for a quick rinse. The last thing I needed right now while trying to get to the bottom of what was going on with Annalyse and struggling to get her back was worrying if Shannon could smell spunk on me.

It was bad enough knowing she saw me with a stauner.

I could die from embarrassment right now if I wasn't so desperate to get Annalyse back. I guess that was some mile marker of evidence that I was breaking free of my ego controlling my every action. So, in some way, there was a small victory to be had from this absolutely mortifying situation.

While I was drying off, I was trying to figure out a way to face Shannon. Half of me wanted to just tell her to leave so I would never have to look her in the eye again, but I needed her help too badly, and, now that I kenned the truth of her connection to this situation, I could not just cast her aside.

I decided that since I had showered, I may as well dress with some fresh clothes, so I grabbed a clean pair of jeans and a t-shirt from the closet and quickly got dressed.

Opening the door, I could hear conversation. Shannon was talking to Jordan in the kitchen. There was, laughter. Did she tell him what happened? I shook my head as I made my way out to meet them.

Right as I rounded the corner the laughing stopped.

Great.

"What's so funny?" I asked, looking between the two of them. They looked like kids who had gotten caught doing something they should not have been.

"Jordan here has been telling me some stories about your childhood. Sounds like you've matured a lot over the years," she said with a smirk.

"Aye. Life will do that to you, I'm afraid." I then turned to Jordan, "I'm sorry, but I need Shannon's help and need to borrow her for a private conversation. Do you mind?"

He simply nodded and made his way out the side doors towards the pool. My guess he was going to go look after the horses for their evening meals.

I turned to look at Shannon and without beating around the bush she simply said, "So you guys had sex? That must be a good sign."

I appreciated her optimism and her maturity about the situation, but I had to set her straight.

"No. *We* didn't have sex. Annalyse and Michael had sex."

"Oh…" she said, obviously confused.

"You told me to tap into that old energy of mine in order to find her by doing so through Michael. I succeeded, but found myself in the middle of a very passionate physical and spiritual energy exchange. As an extension of Michael, I felt what he felt, and, well…."

"Sounds like it was good for him, huh?"

I responded with a raised eyebrow and tight lips.

"Okay, okay. Stop worrying about it. The whole thing makes sense, and you had a normal biological reaction. I'm a mature woman, Henry. Sex isn't something I find to be scandalous or taboo. In fact, I see it as a beautiful act of creation that allows us to tap into our divinity. I'm glad for her that she is feeling well enough to do that."

"What did you just say?" I asked, as I felt anger rising inside me.

"About what?" she asked seeming perplexed by my energy shift.

"About being happy for Annalyse and that she is having sex with Michael." I began pacing around in an attempt to disperse my pent-up energy. "Here I am, alone, trying to figure out how to get her back, and she's just having a good ole time fucking a version of myself that no longer exists!"

265

My breaths heaved in my chest as the fury pulsed through me. This was all too much to bear. I had absolutely no coping method in place for experiencing anything like this. It's like every time I turned around, there was another layer added to this shit cake the universe kept serving up to me.

I was so fucking tired of it.

I kenned everything was happening for a higher purpose, but how much could a one man take? Not only was my beloved taken away from me again, but I now learn that she's in some other spiritual realm making love to a past life version of myself.

"AHHHHGGGG!" I yelled as I knocked everything within reach off the kitchen island and sent it flying across the room.

I leaned on the island counter for a few moments, working to catch my breath and calm myself down before looking up at Shannon.

She was leaning on the other counter looking at me with pursed lips and a raised eyebrow.

"What the fuck was that, Henry?" she asked.

I felt sad for a moment thinking about the contrast between her and Annalyse. If I had had an outburst like that in front of Annalyse, she probably would have gone into a panic attack. My heart clenched with sadness at the thought of having let her down in some way for behaving in that manner.

"Shannon," I said as I hung my head, still leaning on the island. "She's cheating on me with... *me*. Why does she not want me? Why is it *Michael* that she would rather be with?" God, I hated the fact that I was jealous of a past version of myself.

"Here we go again, Henry." Shannon started in on me. "For the love of god, stop making this about you. This is about her. You know what she has been though. You saw for yourself part of it. Her soul has experienced a lot of trauma and *your* soul made an agreement to be there for her, in a safe space, to allow her to heal. You should be happy for her that she feels so safe and secure with Michael to be so open as to make love with him in such a way.

Look at what that part of you is doing for her. Allowing her to find peace and healing when it comes to sexual intimacy though this level of experience. Have you forgotten how much your soul loves her in order for you to have agreed to have left a part of it in this space for her to help her heal? Why have you forgotten what you're doing? Why do you keep going on about this as if it's happening to you? She's with Michael instead of you because his energy is what she needs and yours is not. In order for her to come back to you, your energy is going to have to shift to the level that his is.

You have got to stop focusing on you and putting yourself first. As a complete soul, you loved Annalyse enough to leave behind a part of you for her to hold onto and find solace in, in order for her to find the rest and healing her soul needed so that she could move forward with her destiny. Your destiny. Michael is serving as her guardian, her protector, her safe haven. Do you think she would feel safe, here, with you, now?"

To say that her last statement stung would have been a gross understatement. It was more like I got trapped by a swarm of yellow jackets with nowhere to escape.

I kenned Annalyse would not.

Fuck.

No wonder she would rather be with Michael.

"Look," she said as she walked to the other side of the kitchen island. "You should be grateful to Michael for what he is doing for her. Without him, she would never come back."

"You say that like you know she is coming back," I remarked, as I stared at her poignantly.

Shannon stared at me for a moment before saying, "I do, don't I?"

I scoffed at her remark.

"Is there something you know that I don't? I mean when it comes to this situation. You obviously have a plethora of knowledge that I have no access to."

It was frustrating to think she was holding out on me, though I kenned on some level she was not.

"Henry, what do you believe?" she asked, looking at me imploringly.

I thought for a second.

In truth, I had not stopped for any time since learning Annalyse had returned to her body and was trapped in the astral plane to really think about anything at all besides getting her back and how I could do that.

"I do not ken," I said as I went to sit on the bench at the dining table. "I just want her back."

Shannon took a deep breath as if trying to contend with some impatience that was snaking its way up like kundalini rising.

"This is the very energy that is keeping you trapped in your own suffering. Why can't you just see? There is nothing wrong here. Nothing. Annalyse's soul experienced a trauma, and she is needing time to rehabilitate, and she's having to do that with a part of you that is in balance. You're looking at this all wrong. As if something is wrong and it's not. If you broke your arm, would you stare at it day in and day out trying to 'figure out' how to fix it?

No. You would trust your body and know that it is doing what it needs to do to heal. On its own time. Staring at it, trying to make it be healed, would only make the process take longer because you would be putting additional stress on your body instead of allowing it the energy it needs to repair itself. You must remember that you two are one and the same when it comes to your soul. When yours is in turmoil so is hers. It's your need to try to control the situation that is prolonging your suffering. Nothing else."

Fuck.

How the hell was Shannon so wise? I wondered to myself how many lifetimes she had experienced and how many she had been in with me. I also wondered if she remembered any more of them than the last one where Annalyse and I were together as Michael and Sara. She seemed to be on some next level that I could not possibly think to aspire to. Her point struck me hard, and it finally clicked.

I looked up at her and said, "So you're telling me that Annalyse will only wake up when I have found peace in the loss of her?"

Shannon closed her eyes and leaned her head back as if she would be looking up at the ceiling and took a deep breath. After lowering her head back down she looked at me and said, "You're getting there, but you're still not quite all the way. You are seeing yourself in separation. Thinking and reacting as if the two of you are separate and apart." She cocked her head to the side slightly and stared at me imploringly. "Can you separate your own soul Henry? We thought so, when we first started this, but then quickly learned that the souls were not actually separated, their connection was simply deeply hidden, but it was still there. Even when you yourself travel through the astral planes or leave a peace of it in a past life for another to find; is it truly possible for you be apart from yourself in such a way? It's not, the soul may be in a different time, space reality, but it is still yours."

She paused for a moment then added, "I wish you would understand. It's not what *is* that is the problem, it's how you *feel* about it."

I thought more for a few moments, allowing her words to fully move through my cognitive system and be processed and sorted appropriately. Then it was as if someone had slid a missing puzzle piece into its empty slot, and everything began falling into place.

"Oh, Shannon...." I let my words trail off thanks to the pain in my chest that was making it almost impossible to breathe. My head hung with the weight of my heartache.

She walked over to sit down next to me and said, "Ah, I think we are there."

"Aye," I said nodding my head lightly. "As long as I feel in separation, there will be separation, like when Annalyse and I had both hidden our soul connection from each other, but when I can get back into the alignment of wholeness and connectedness, that is when she will also."

"Piece of cake right," she said sarcastically.

I gave out a light chuckle in response.

In truth, it seemed like the hardest fucking thing I'd ever have to do in my entire existence.

How does one feel "connected" to someone who is obviously not here? How do I *feel* she is here while staring at her lifeless body?

I felt like what she just told me might have been the equivalent of someone gay being told to just not be gay or telling someone straight to be gay. How do I change who I am and how I feel? At least for me, the feelings in question, here, with me, were reprogrammable. I guess that was something.

"Henry, try to help me understand why you are still struggling here. It's like you're worried that she won't do what you both planned for her to do."

I could tell Shannon was getting frustrated again with me. I honestly did not blame her. Letting go of Annalyse was the hardest goddamn thing I have ever had to do. She was a piece of me. I feared what I would become if I lost that part of myself.

Who would I be?

"I wish I kenned how to explain it. I wish I could...." My words faded off, as I struggled to put them together in a way that would articulate the fear and anguish I was experiencing. But there were no words. Sometimes there are things that happen to us that are so deep, so dark, and so painful that words cannot describe them. Words are things we use to create things. Books, spells – even the word "spelling" came from the concept of stringing words together to make something come into existence – and stories were all just made up of words, and, when those words come together, they could create other worlds, other realities, and even speak life or death into someone's hopes and dreams. No matter how powerful they were, words could not be used to convey certain feelings and experiences. It's just not possible for something that is used for creation to breathe life into something so inert and void as the depth of my fear and hopelessness.

I could tell Shannon could see my rising frustrations and stress, as I grappled to explain what I was going through.

"Look," she said. "It is the natural state of creation and nature for things to grow. When things are left unhindered and simply allowed to do what they were designed to do, they grow. It's when they are stifled or cut down that the natural cycle is disrupted and the growth stops. Henry, you're trying to put Annalyse in a box. Not only does she not fit, but by you trying to force her to your will, you are preventing her from growing. She will not be able to step into who she truly is until you stop trying to make her be something you think she should be and allow her to become what she truly is."

I kenned she was right. Why was this so difficult?

Every time I tried to let go, every time I thought I had let go, something happened to show me that there was another level to the release.

"Hey," she said, bumping my shoulder with hers, "At least you were able to energetically bond with her this time."

I looked over at her in confusion. "What do you mean?"

"Sex," she said matter-of-factly. "Annalyse may have thought she was connecting with Michael in that way, but it was this," she shoved her thumb in my direction, "version of you that she was actually connecting with in that moment. That was probably the first time she has ever experienced a union with you while you were in your entirety. That's a big step because in that moment it wasn't 'Michael' who was helping her heal. It was you. The version of you that has reassimilated Michael."

My eyes danced around as I processed this information. Her point was valid, as usual, and it made me feel a lot better to realize what she was telling me.

Looking at her I asked, "Do you think it would be easier to connect with her now that we have a new energetic cord?"

"Yes, Henry, I do. You formed a very powerful one with her just now. Maybe we should start to tug on it a bit?"

I was shocked by her words. She had been the one telling me to take it easy. Guiding me to not push or force anything. Now she was suggesting that I energetically tug on Annalyse as a means to what?

Find her again, or pull her out of this place she was seeking refuge in?

"Shannon, am I hearing you correctly? You are actually encouraging me to pull on this energetic tether? How and for what ends?"

"Well, let's look at this for a moment. The first time we made it in, we had to create an energetic portal in order the try to find her. Which I'm sure you remember, was daunting."

I scoffed at her statement.

Daunting?

It was downright formidable. I had felt like I was in a remake of *The Craft*.

Shannon had sat quietly for a while to meditate. I had never seen someone meditate in this way. Her eyes danced behind her eyelids and her body twitched as if she had been having a nightmare. By the time she opened her eyes, I was already feeling out of my depth and a bit trepidatious about our next step.

"Alright, Henry, grab some pillows and lay down on the floor. Here," she had said, and pointed to a rather large space of floor in my bedroom. I did as she asked, wondering what she had in store, as she left the room for a moment.

When she came back, she had a pad of paper that she had started drawing symbols on and a bag.

Oh Christ....

I had silently watched as she had placed pieces of paper around me in a geometric pattern. Upon closer inspection, these pieces of paper had strange symbols on them.

"What are those?" I asked as she began taking crystals out of her bag.

"They are light language codes that I just received during meditation. These crystals will help to amplify them and keep us from getting lost in the space where Annalyse is."

Oh....

I had so many questions, but I could tell it was not the time to ask them.

"Go ahead and lay back," she said as she brushed her hand in the air gesturing me to lay down.

To my surprise, she laid down next to me.

"Hold my hand, Henry," was the last thing she said to me before we found ourselves in the black.

It was the space that held the doors. Only this time, I could see them better. It was as if some black mist hung in the air like the shadow of something that could not be seen. It was still dark, but navigable.

"Well, it looks like you were right," Shannon remarked while looking around. "Facing your shadow has helped lift some of it from this space."

"Here!" I exclaimed. "Here is the door where I felt Annalyse."

As I had reached for the handle, I had hesitated.

Shannon touched my arm and said, "Hey, you can do this. Just feel her...."

I nodded and then took a deep breath. I then closed my eyes and imagined her in front of me. I pictured us happy and smiling at one another. I allowed the joy the fill me. While holding this image, and with my eyes still closed, I had placed both hands on the door and it easily pushed open.

I opened my eyes and looked over at Shannon in astonishment.

"I knew you could do it," she had said.

What we had found on the other side of the door was not what either of us expected.

There was nothing.

It was just plain white. Everywhere.

"I do not understand," I said to Shannon as we looked around.

"I think I do," she responded. "It's a blank slate. This is where she is creating her reality. I think you are meant to create one for her. There is something here that she needs to know but doesn't know to access or seek it."

Shannon closed her eyes for a moment and then added, "Yes. Oh, you clever girl...."

It was then that Shannon helped me project the beautiful pool surrounded by trees where we then had our first encounter with Annalyse.

"This time," Shannon continued, bringing me back to the present, "you didn't connect with Annalyse's energy. You finally tapped into Michael's." She paused for a moment and then added, "Oh my goddess, Henry. We have been going about this all the wrong way. We knew this from the beginning, but we lost focus – which is understandable, as this is a very challenging obstacle course to navigate – but now we know that we were right all along. These last few weeks, we have been so focused on trying to tap into Annalyse's energy, when in fact, *you're already there*."

As her words washed over me, I could feel a coldness spread across my skin as if I had been covered in sweat and stepped out into the freezing temperature outside. I ducked my head down and ran both my hands through my hair.

Dear God. She was right. Here I was doing it again. Focusing on fixing her, instead of working on myself. It was my own integration that I needed to focus on. But how?

"Henry, stop. I already know what you're thinking, and there is no need to get all in your head like you do."

I looked up and gave her a glare which she met with a raised eyebrow and pursed lips as if to say, "Try me."

"Okay then, Shannon. Please. Since you ken all, please tell me what I must do now."

"We need to do a past life regression and process the pain and loss that Michael experienced, once and for all."

I let my head drop back and stared at the ceiling.

Of course, we do. Great.

CHAPTER 16
Henry

After Shannon and I decided it would be best for me to wait until the next day to do the past life regression, since I was not in the mental space to move forward with that type of work immediately, Shannon made her way home, and I went to clear my head with some sword swinging with Jordan.

Several hours of sword slinging rendered my muscles practically useless. It was just past eleven o'clock at night, and I kenned I needed to get some rest for what we had planned tomorrow afternoon.

While showering, I replayed the plans Shannon and I had developed some hours earlier.

We had decided that tomorrow afternoon would be a better time to do my past life regression. As Aine had been studying them so extensively for Annalyse before Annalyse had been forced out of

Vivien's body, we concluded that it would be best to utilize her knowledge to perform the regression for me.

Shannon wanted us to go back to the lifetime that Annalyse and I both had memories from. Mine I had used to inspire my last book *The Path to Redemption* without having realized that they were actual memories I was seeing flash in my mind. I had simply thought it was just another story that was coming together.

I was nervous to go back to that time, especially now that I kenned for sure that those were actual memories resurfacing, which I had shared on paper as they had bubbled their way up to my conscious mind. It was a very painful time for both Annalyse and myself. My body quivered slightly under the warm running water as I could feel the nervous tension trying to escape. How there could be any latent energy trapped anywhere in my body was incredible to me.

At least I would see Annalyse in the morning before going into this traumatic space. It shook me to think about reexperiencing any of that loss, gore, and pain, but if it was what I needed to do to help Annalyse, then it was what I would do.

There was no question on that.

I took a deep breath and ducked my head under the flow of the water that now cascaded down my head, face, and back. I allowed the warmth to wash away all my fears and reminded myself that what I would be witnessing was like watching a movie, and I simply needed to stay in observation mode instead of aligning with what was happening – at least that is what Aine said I would need to do.

Another thing on this journey that should be no problem, right?

Shutting the water off snapped me out of my head and back into my body. I quickly got myself dressed – though it was a challenge as my muscles quaked with almost every movement I made – and got myself ready for bed.

I was practically asleep before my head made contact with the pillow.

I woke up the next morning to see a big, fluffy face peering at me.

I had been sleeping on my side, facing the space where Annalyse belonged, and instead of seeing her beautiful face when I awoke, I saw that of Sunshine, her rather large and fluffy orange cat. He looked as if he were hatching an egg, with his paws tucked up underneath his body, and stared at me with slow blinks.

Utilizing the arm that I was not laying on, I pet his soft, ginger head, and as if there had been a power switch there, it immediately activated his purring center.

"Good morning, great beast," I said to him. "I will feed you and then get myself ready to be off to see our favorite girl. We have big plans today."

Just reminding myself of what we had planned today made my stomach flip.

I checked my watch before climbing out of bed. It was about seven-thirty in the morning. By the time I had gotten Sunshine fed, had a quick rinse in the shower, and gotten dressed, the clock in the dash of my vehicle said it was two minutes before eight o'clock.

When I got to the hospital, I was surprised to see how quiet everything was. There was typically more action in the hallways. The peace made me hopeful that today might continue in that trajectory.

As I entered Annalyse's room, I saw that Morgan was stirring around and getting herself ready to leave.

"Morning," I said to her with a nod of acknowledgement.

"So?" was her response.

"I am sorry?" I said, feeling confused.

"Did it work? Were you able to make contact with her yesterday?"

Oh Christ!

I had been so caught up in what had happened and our plans for today that I had forgotten to tell Morgan what had happened when I went back in to try to make contact with Annalyse.

"Oh, Morgan, forgive me," I began, as I walked closer to her so I could lower my voice while speaking to her. "Aye, I did indeed make contact. It was different than the time before and she was more open to connecting with me," I did not see the need to go into details. "But clearly I could not get her to come back yet."

Morgan stood in front of me and nodded in response.

She was clearly thinking and processing what I had just told her. I began getting nervous that she would press me for more details. Fortunately, she did not ask for more information, but what she did ask for was a lot more significant.

"I want to be there next time," she said.

My first reaction was to say, "Absolutely not," but I held my tongue. I kenned that she had been feeling left out, and I did not want her to feel that way anymore. I also did not want her to be in the same room with me when I woke up after just ejaculating on myself in my sleep.

I could feel chagrin spreading up my cheeks as I thought about it.

Morgan was clearly watching my body language and could tell I was uncomfortable with this plan and that I was having a mental battle between the two options.

"Please, Henry," she said with a softness that I had kenned she possessed but had never shown to me.

What the hell? I thought. At this point, what did it matter? I was about as raw and exposed as I would ever be, so what was the difference in adding one more person to my deep, emotional processing.

I let out a deep breath and said, "Actually Morgan, it so happens that Shannon will be coming over later to help me with a past life regression in hopes that it might help me develop my connection more with Annalyse. You are welcome to join us if you would like."

Morgan looked uncertain about this idea, and I remembered Annalyse telling me that Morgan was more religious than Annalyse was. I worried I may have made Morgan feel too uncomfortable about this notion.

"It is entirely up to you," I added in hopes of letting her ken that I did not want her doing something that she did not feel comfortable doing.

She stayed quiet for another moment or two and then said, "Actually, I would like that. It is a bit outside of my comfort zone, but I have had to acknowledge that there is something more at work here that I don't understand, so I am open to learning more if it can help Annalyse."

Part of me was pleased that she accepted my invitation, while the other part squirmed with anxiety at the thought of having another audience member present for my possible, future humiliation.

"Alright then," I said. "Shannon plans to come by around one o'clock this afternoon. I can text you the address."

"Okay," she said in response, as she gathered up her belongings into her arms and began walking towards the door. "I will run home, freshen up, check in with the office, and then head over."

Just as she was walking out the door she looked back and added, "And Henry? Thank you."

I simply nodded in response, "See you at one."

Once she was through the door, I looked at Annalyse and said to her, "Oh my neach-gaoil, is there nothing I would not do for you?"

The truth was, that is why I agreed to let Morgan join us in our efforts of getting to Annalyse. I kenned that is what she would have wanted.

The hours flew by in a whirl of remembering to text Jordan to say I would be training with him later that night instead of the afternoon, doing my usual massage work for Annalyse, and even jotting down some notes for my next book.

Sooner than I expected it to feel, I was back in my own bed, lying down with Morgan and Shannon seated in chairs next to me.

To say I was terrified was an understatement, but there was nothing more I wanted in this world than to be back in physical union with Annalyse. So, if this was another monster of mine that I had to slay to get to her, then there was no question of whether I would charge it down, sword out.

"You ready?" said Shannon.

I wanted to say, "Fuck no," but something I have learned in my life was that one of the most challenging things to do, when going full force after your dreams, is to not talk yourself out of doing it.

So I turned my head and looked her square in the eyes and said, "Aye. I am ready."

Shannon nodded and then looked at Morgan, who shrugged in response, before turning her attention to Aine.

"Aine," she began. "Take Henry back to where it all started."

My body quivered as Aine responded and began the process of sending me back to my own personal hell.

There was smoke everywhere.

I coughed and choked as I tried getting closer to what was left of my home.

It had been burned to ash.

My body was so tired from the long journey and the only think that had kept me going was the thought of seeing my dearest Sarah and to meet our child.

When I came riding over the hill to see our home in a smoldering heap on the ground I felt as if my heart had fallen out of my chest and lodged itself in my stomach.

"He-ya!" I had yelled at my horse, kicking his sides, forcing him to go faster.

As I rode upon the scene of destruction, I heaved my leg over top of my horse and jumped off him sideways while he was still at a gallop. When I hit the ground, I pushed my body with every bit of adrenaline I had left to run as fast as my legs would carry me – towards the pain I would never have imagined.

I slowed my pace as I approached what was left of the wooden front door that was hanging mangled and charred. Smoke still curled off the wood, as if it were a ghost denying entry to any who may come. I held my arm up to my face trying to use the inner part of my elbow to shield my nose and mouth from the smoke.

It was when I went to take a step forward that I heard something to the side of the house.

"Sara!" I yelled as I set of at a run.

It was when I rounded the corner that I saw her.

My dearest Sara, lying on the ground, clutching the body of a small child.

"Get! Get out of here!" I yelled to the birds who had been picking at their charred, decaying bodies. The birds must have been what had made the noise that grabbed my attention and lead me to this gruesome sight.

Stepping closer, I could see what was left of the two lives that had made the last few years of my own life worth fighting to keep – and there was no life left in them. The hope that had kept me going was gone.

Sara, and what looked like a young girl, by what I could tell of the remains of her dress, lay on the ground, barely identifiable as they had been burned almost beyond recognition.

I collapsed on the ground next to them and let out a guttural scream of rage and pain. It ripped through my throat like the pain that was ripping through every nerve in my body.

All I could do was look at them. I could not touch them or hold them because of the state of their condition. I could merely peer at the grotesque result of hatred that caused my beloved and my dear sweet little girl so much pain.

For what may have been mere moments or several hours, I remained on my knees. I was transfixed by the macabre scene before me, and, finding that I was now numb to the pain of the loss I had discovered, a new emotion was beginning to fill me. I could feel it pouring through my body like a magical transfiguration potion. I could feel my muscles strengthening. I could feel my heart pounding and there was no sound but the roaring inside my own head.

Aye. I had moved past the pain and discovered a new feeling on which I was fast becoming drunk.

Rage.

I pushed myself up to my feet and whistled for my horse, who came galloping over.

After mounting up, I gave my girls one last look and said, "I will be back," and then took off for the town.

The sun was beginning to set just as I road into town. What the people were not expecting was that soon the ground would match the red that was gently being cast over it.

I kenned what they had done, and I kenned why they did it, and now I was their Angel of Death coming to claim their lives, just like they took those of Sara and my little girl, whose name I did not even ken.

There was a reason I was so feared.

I was a warrior. I was one of the most deadly men that walked the earth. How foolish they were to think they could get away with such wretched evil against me.

They saw me coming, as I rode in like an apocalyptic demon, and they began to scatter and flee.

It made no difference.

I would find them all, and I would destroy them.

I kenned who were the ones responsible, and I kenned just where to find them.

There was no hiding.

As I galloped up to the front of the church, I charged my horse into the sanctuary.

The irony cast a sickening half grin across my face. Sanctuary? More like prison. These people were the worst kinds of hypocrites. Pretending to practice the love of Jesus, while contorting the words of the Bible into whatever bile suited them in the moment in order to cause fear, so that they could control the people and murder any that they could not.

Will they never learn?

People do not want to be controlled – and personally, I was sick of it.

I fought for a failed cause simply because I hoped it would protect my family, only to learn that, because I fought, they died a hideous and gruesome death. In my deluded effort to protect them, I became responsible for their death.

Father McGinter stood staring at me, transfixed. I was certain I looked like an avenging angel, as the sun set directly behind me, illuminating my silhouette against the orange sky.

"What is the meaning of this?" he half shouted and half stuttered as his throat convulsed with fear.

"You tell me, Father McGinter. What is the meaning of this?" I asked while pointing at the cross that hung on the wall straight ahead of me. "Certainly not love, or compassion, or," I swung my leg over my horse and hopped down to the ground, "acceptance, is it?"

"Michael?" he asked as he squinted against the bright light coming in through the open doors.

"Aye," I answered as I pulled my sword from its sheath.

Father McGinter slowly began backing away.

"We – we thought you were dead," he stammered while he continued to fumble his way backwards.

I laughed at his cowardice. How sickening. To be responsible for the deaths of an innocent woman and child yet fear death yourself?

"Am I not?" I asked as I continued to slowly stalk my prey.

"Look, Michael, you must understand. The evidence against them was irrefutable," he said as his back hit the wall. "We had no choice!" he added shrilly.

"No?" I asked calmly as I stood feet from him. "And what kind of evidence did you have?"

"Greer had come forward with some very damning evidence against Sara and even Rose."

I faltered for a moment.

Rose.

The rage began to pump through my body again, as the pain of kenning that I would never have the joy of meeting my dear Rose because this malevolent man ordered her to be tortured and murdered based on lies.

I found it ironic that the woman whom I declined affections from multiples times, and who had always fancied me, would be the one who so happened to have discovered damning evidence against the woman that she saw as an obstacle to get to me.

"You are a fool Father, and your soul is as damned as your witness."

Just then I noticed the shadow of a man silently approaching me from behind with a sword raised. I *spun on my heels and swung my sword around, cleanly removing his head from his body.*

With the distraction, Father McGinter made a run for it. I knelt down and unsheathed the dagger I kept at my ankle and sent it flying. It found its mark with accuracy, planting itself at the base of his skull. The force of my throw sending the dagger straight through his neck so that the point stuck out the front of his throat.

He fell hard, face first into the grass.

I walked over to him, looking down on him like the filth that he was, then, using my foot, rolled him over onto his side.

He was still alive.

Good.

I squatted down to get closer to his face, and, tilting my head to one side as if to study him, said, "There is a special hell waiting just for you. You did not kill witches, Father McGinter. You killed women and children. The only evil that has been walking this earth is you. And now the last thing you will see before you meet your judgment are the eyes of a man who was always a far greater threat to you than any woman or child could have ever been."

He coughed and gaged as he choked on his own blood. As far as I was concerned, he was drowning in all the blood he was responsible for spilling.

Once the light went out in his eyes, I stood up to walk away and said, "And you can keep the dagger. I will not be needing it."

As I made my way to my horse, I kenned I had two choices: finish my vengeance or go be with my wife and child.

I was beginning to feel my exhaustion again, and I decided that I was ready to rest.

Mounting up, I told my horse, "Let us go home."

After we arrived, I lead my faithful beast to the stables, removed his bridle and saddle, and gave his bottom a swift pop. He took off into the field.

I let out a deep sigh, "Enjoy your freedom, beast. I ken I will."

Slowly, I made my way back over to the house and kicked the remnants of the front door down. Shielding my nose and mouth again with my arm, I made my way through the desecration, eventually making my way up to the same balcony I had assumed Sara had thrown herself off, while clutching Rose in her arms.

I made my way up to the gap between the stones and looked down on their bodies. It was nearly dark now, and, in the low light, it almost looked as if they were simply sleeping.

That is how I would remember them.

I climbed up onto the stone and closed my eyes, picturing the two of them lying together, peaceful and happy in a loving embrace. A faint smile touched my lips, as a tear made its way out of my closed eye, onto my cheek.

With a deep breath, I leaned over and fell to join my beloveds, holding this perfectly beautiful scene in my mind.

When I opened my eyes, I was shocked to find myself surrounded by white.

Everything was white.

I stood up, looked around, and began shouting, "Sara! Rose!" But heard nothing in response. The silence was disturbing and unnerving.

There was a white mist hovering around me that felt safe and comforting and helped ease the panic I was beginning to feel. I had no idea where I was or what this space was, but I very quickly became comfortable with the idea of being here. It was as if the mist was some type of potion that hung in the air with the goal of calming me.

It was just as I was beginning to feel very relaxed and at peace that a bright figure began making its way through the mist.

"Sara?" I asked, as I squinted through the haze.

"No, Michael, I am not Sara," said a gentle female voice. "I am Archangel Azrael. I am here to support you in your transition."

"My transition?" I asked.

"Yes, dear one. You have exited the physical plain and are now reentering the ethereal. This space," she gestured around with one of her hands, "is designed to help your spirit acclimate, by helping your vibration rise to a more compatible state, before reconnecting fully with your soul's true essence."

There was a part of me that had no idea what she was talking about, and then another part that felt that her answer was completely valid and acceptable.

"I think we are about there?" she asked as the mist slowly began to dissolve away.

As it did so, details of the room I was in were starting to come into being. I was standing in a large cavern that looked as if it were made out of some clear stone. There was a large pool in the center that was filled with a pale purple looking substance.

Turning my head, I was surprised to see a group of, what I could only call people, standing at the side of the room. I called them people, though some did not look human at all. As my eyes moved from one face to another they froze when they landed on a familiar-looking one.

"Sara!" I shouted as I began running towards her.

"No, Michael, I am not Sara," she said while bringing her hands up in front of her body as a sign to tell me to slow down. "My name is Theia. I am Sara's oversoul."

I stepped back in shock.

"Well then, where is Sara?" I asked.

"She has already moved on."

"Moved on? Moved on where?"

"She has already reincarnated into a new life experience to prepare for the work the two of you must do next time you reunite."

This information cut me deeply. I felt a deep ache in my sternum, as if someone had punched me from the inside.

"Michael, I understand that now this seems painful, but as you continue to reintegrate you will begin to understand." She said this while gesturing me towards the pool.

I looked at her in confusion.

"You want me to go swimming?" I asked.

A patient smile tugged at her lips. "It's not for swimming. Once you enter the Iserus you will begin integrating the information much more quickly and clearly."

Not kenning what other option I had at the moment, I made my way over to the pool that she had referred to as "Iserus" and began removing my clothes. I did not see the point in getting embarrassed, since part of me thought this was all probably just a dream anyway.

When I touched the surface of the fluid, it did not feel like anything. It was not hot or cold. It did not even feel wet. It simply was.

After realizing I was not going to boil or freeze, I walked straight into the pool until the substance was up to my chin.

"Do I need to go under?" I called out.

"No," said a voice from behind me.

Standing at the edge of the pool was a very familiar man: me.

"What in the name of Christ?" I said as I began making my way back over to the edge.

Once I had climbed back out and put my clothes back on, I stood directly in front of myself.

Looking at Theia I asked, "And who is this?"

"Don't you know?" she asked in reply.

Turning my attention back to the man who looked just like me I said, "Is he my over soul?" as I examined his features.

He smiled at me and said, "Yes, Michael. My name is Ky and we have a lot to discuss. Please," he gestured over to a table that looked as if it were made from the same materials as the cavern that was surrounded with matching chairs.

Ky and Theia began to tell me about Sara's and my mission. About our role in the collective and the work that was laid out before us. There were times during the conversation where I thought I truly must be dreaming and others when I wished I was. What they were talking about seemed so very overwhelming and impossible.

"Why would we ever have agreed to do this?" I asked.

"Love," was the answer they both gave at the exact same time.

"We wanted to save our people," Ky added.

"And we still do," said Theia.

I nodded in understanding.

"Aye, so what do I need to do now?" I asked.

Ky and Theia looked at each other uncertainly before answering. This did not seem to bode well for me. I squirmed slightly in my seat.

Ky answered, "In the next lifetime where you and Sara find each other and come together in a physical union, she is going to need a spiritual safe haven for her to heal and process some very extreme trauma."

I suddenly became aware of my heart feeling like it was being squeezed.

Had she not already been through so much?

Taking a deep breath, I asked, "How do I do this for her? How will I be able to help her?"

Theia answered this time.

"She will seek you out, and it is imperative that she find you. It is the only way for both of you to fulfill your mission."

"Okay. But how will she be able to find me as Michael if I am reincarnated as someone else in a different lifetime?"

"Well," began Ky. "This is the most challenging part. You will need to split your spirit so that you can leave part of it behind so that she can find it."

I sat back in my chair, "Split my spirit?"

"Aye," Ky replied.

"That sounds…. Painful."

Theia looked at me with compassion and said, "It is said to be agony."

I brought my hands up to my face and let my hand support my head while I let out a deep sigh. Then lifting my head, I looked between the two of them and asked, "When do we start?"

"Whenever you're ready," Ky replied.

I stood up as a way of letting them ken I was ready now. Following my lead, they both stood up from the table and began guiding me over to another table that looked similar to the one we left but was designed for someone to lay on top of.

"Lay down," Theia instructed.

I did as I was told, wondering how painful "agony" would be.

My fearful thoughts were interrupted by the white cat-like creature that came over to my bedside and began hovering its hand over my chest.

Afraid to watch, I closed my eyes, but even with them closed, I could see an incredibly bright light begin growing from my chest.

Just when my curiosity got the best of me and I thought to open my eyes, I felt it.

It was like no other pain I had ever experienced before because it was not a physical pain. It felt like part of my identity was being stolen away and being placed in a dark box, hidden away from me. It was as if I were in hell – complete separation from my source.

I opened my eyes to see that the light had gone out and the cat-like creature was placing the lid on what appeared to be a white vial that contained pure light.

"How do you feel?" Theia asked.

I took a breath only to realize that it did not quite satisfy. It was as if there was as open hole somewhere in my chest, allowing all my life force to slip through it.

Looking up at her, I responded.

"I feel empty."

She nodded and put a hand on my shoulder. "It's only temporary, and, once you reincarnate, you won't know any different. Humans are used to feeling separated from their souls."

I nodded.

The truth was, without Sara, I was already empty. What was carving out the hole a little bigger?

"Ten, nine, eight...."

Huh? The room was beginning to fill with mist again.

"You are now starting to become aware of your physical surroundings. Seven... six... five..."

This was when I realized, Aine was waking bringing me out of my regression.

"Four... three... two..."

And just as I was about to open my eyes, I was pulled back under.

CHAPTER 17

I absolutely loved everything about this place. My favorite thing, though, was the large tree that stood in the middle of the field behind our house. It was a lone tree that stood out amongst the flat ground that led to the cliff just beyond. It was one of those magical, majestic trees that looked like it could contain all knowledge.

It was tall, with beautiful branches that spread out in all directions, creating a canopy of green and gold as the leaves mixed with the sunlight, and they danced in the breeze, causing a sparkling effect while they moved together in harmony. Perhaps it was a tree like this that gave name to the Tree of Life in the Bible. Perhaps it wasn't the fruit that gave the gift of knowledge, but the tree itself. Maybe by consuming a part of the tree, Adam and Eve became one with it and its DNA, and it became part of theirs. Could it be that by consuming the fruit of the tree, it didn't actually "open their eyes" but instead, it woke them up? By partaking of the Tree of Life, could it be that perhaps they remembered their own true self?

What a fascinating thing to ponder as I walked around my beloved, and very own, Tree of Life. I wondered to myself if that had been a choice – to live in peace and harmony but never grow, change or evolve, or to experience pain and suffering and grow as a result of it. I imagined Adam and Eve living together, happily, peacefully, with nothing changing yet everything seeming fine. This thought gave me a pang of discomfort. The idea, as intoxicating as it was, seemed unenticing to me. It sounded like prison. It almost seemed as if it was a lie and the characters had all been painted in a warped view.

It was as if Adam and Eve had actually been held captive, in some way, by a force that promised them peace and that they would be taken care of, but at the sacrifice of their freedom. Then here came the snake telling them that it was all a lie. That by surrendering their freedom, yes, their life was peaceful and fine, but they would and could never grow, they could never be more, they could never access the power and knowledge of god, himself, until they made the choice to do so.

The snake didn't lie. It just took the snake thousands of years and thousands of physical experiences to gain the knowledge, and it wanted to share it with others. The snake was not the enemy, he was an activator.

I loved coming to spend time with the tree. Walking alone, barefoot, to the swing Michael had constructed for me, I would swing for what felt like hours, watching the house, or facing out towards the cliffs, to watch the sun set. My tree allowed me all of this, and I always felt a deep connection to it, as if being close to it, I could tap into its own rootedness which would then bring me closer to my loving Mother Gaia.

Today was another beautiful day. It felt like everything here was just perfect. Always. It was my very own Eden.

I sat on my swing and began my flight. There was something so freeing about swinging. I felt weightless as if I were floating and flying through the air. I closed my eyes and fully gave myself over to the sensation. The wind kissed at my face as the warm sunlight bathed it in its golden glow. Yes, this was my very own Eden, or maybe even heaven itself.

After opening my eyes, I noticed Michael had made his way out to tend to his duties around the property. As I watched Michael work in the field, I felt so peaceful, but there was something that felt unsettling. It was almost as if things were too perfect, and I kept having this nagging feeling like there was something I was forgetting.

It was as if the information kept trying to come through, but there was some wall in my mind keeping it out. Michael had started worrying about me, worrying that I wasn't happy. I was. Very much so, but I just couldn't shake this feeling.

I wondered if at some time my own serpent would show up and tell me of a truth that would tear away my own Eden. Part of me feared this, while another invited the knowledge. I had come to realize that happiness and contentment were two very different feelings. I was happy, but I wasn't content. I wasn't satisfied. My soul was craving something more. I just couldn't remember what.

Purpose?

I could tell that the sun was starting to go down, so I turned in my swing to get a better view so I could watch it as it passed by the edge of the cliff and set underneath the line of where the earth ended. I'd watched this almost every day since I'd woken up with Michael. There was a part of me that always wondered why I had no real memory of the time before waking up next to him, though I hadn't cared much to even wonder about it since I was so comfortable.

But was I?

I felt agitated, like my soul had gotten it's fill of what it needed and was ready to move on... to what?

And that's where the cycle of thought kept coming and going. I tried not to pay much mind to it. It felt so good to be in a space where I had little to no worries, felt loved and adored by the man of my dreams, and simply felt at peace, but the sense of peace was wearing off as each day went by and was replaced with anticipation. I felt like my picture-perfect world was slowly unraveling in some way. I felt restless.

I felt like something was coming.

It seemed as if the earth was feeling the same way. The ground began moving in an almost quivering fashion. I stopped pumping my legs on the swing and slowly brought myself to a stop so that I could better make out what was happening.

As I stood up I could I feel energy bubbling up inside me that needed to be released. It almost felt uncomfortable, which surprised me. I was always comfortable here. Discomfort was a foreign thing to me; an awareness but not an actual experience.

Until now.

I could feel the ache inside my chest. Something needed to get out.

Just as I could begin to feel this energy build up inside of my chest, I began seeing little creatures crawling along the ground, making their way towards me. This must have been what was causing the grass to move in such a way that made it seem like the ground was quivering.

It was difficult to make them out. My eyes strained to see them in the changing light cast by the setting sun, and, as I watched, I began feeling afraid, angry, and defensive. It was almost as if I was feeling what these creatures were feeling.

I couldn't believe that I was seeing such a thing in my perfect world that I lived so peacefully in. As I stood in the middle of the field with all these wounded creatures, I began to realize that they weren't malicious. They were injured.

No, that wasn't the right way to describe it.

They were *unhealed*.

As they drew closer, I could feel the pressure growing inside me. It was becoming almost unbearable to hold it in. But I wanted to. I wanted them to come closer so that I could decipher what they looked like – until finally I could get a glimpse of them.

They were repulsive.

But not in the typical way one would think. My heart ached for them. They looked almost like small, starving children who were covered in black tar that had caused their skin to turn leathery and tight against their protruding bones. Their skin reminded me of what a bat's wing looked like.

Their bodies were covered in oddly-shaped wounds. I could feel a pang in my stomach as I responded to what I perceived their pain must have felt like.

That's when it happened. It was like that pang was a spark to ignite an explosion.

BOOM!

The relief.

A shockwave of light and energy exploded from my chest, sending all the creatures scampering and running away to hide in the woods, seek refuge behind rocks, and cower in the tall grass.

I stood, with my hands rested on my knees, breathing deeply, almost panting for air. I felt so much relief from letting the build up of energy out and releasing it into the cosmos and beyond.

Once I got my breath, I looked around for the macabre looking creatures. It was easier to see them, now as I was radiating light in all directions. Behind rocks and at the edge of the tree line that led into the forest, I could see them cowering. They seemed terrified. Feeling sorry for them, I began moving towards them before hearing my own voice in my head.

"Do not follow them. They cannot go where you go."

I found this puzzling. I watched them from a distance as they hid and cowered, trying to understand their behavior. As I moved, so did my light. When the light hit their wounds, the wounds would glisten, as if they had electricity moving through them, and the creature would cry out and hide again. That's when I realized that it wasn't that they were afraid of me, it was that they were afraid of my light and what it did when it shone onto their wounds.

I felt so sad for them.

I could tell that the light was healing to them, but it was almost as if they didn't want to be healed. The electricity in the wound was the energy of healing, and in order for them to heal the wounds, they would have to bring them into the light. How incredible to realize how terrifying that was for them. It seemed as if they would rather suffer their whole existence and live a half-life of pain and suffering instead of allowing the light to expose the wounds so they could be healed.

What?

How was suffering with a wounding preferred over healing it so one could move forward?

Just as the information resonated, I heard the same voice again. "They are not ready."

Ah... I thought.

Then I chose to simply honor their journey because, in that moment, I remembered that there was a time that I too wasn't ready to heal and let go either.

And this is when I realized that, like them, I was still hiding.

I took a deep breath and closed my eyes. When I opened them, I noticed that the sky was beautiful and orange and there were streaks of pink and purple that were reflecting off the clouds that appeared to be holding up the sky at the edge of the world.

As I was taking in the wonderment of the colors, I noticed something strange on the horizon. It appeared as if a man were walking towards me. A man who had just appeared at the edge of the cliff, as if it truly were the edge of the world. *My* world.

I remained still and watched as the dark shadow of a figure, that was contrasted by the light behind it, slowly made its way towards me. I felt as if my own light might be hampering my ability to clearly see the figure that was coming into form, so I worked to connect my breath to it and brought it down by taking slow, deep breaths. My light had become fully contained just as I began to make out a man's features.

He was tall and well built, and, as the orange sun hit his hair, it made it look as if it was comprised of flames. His style of dress was strange. It looked odd, as it didn't look like what Michael and I wore. The shirt had buttons and the shoes did not look as if they would be good for working on the land. His pants looked strange, as if they were made from some blue material that felt oddly familiar to me, though I had no memory of having seen it before.

As he continued to approach, I realized that I had no fear of this man. There was something unusually recognizable about him, and I knew intuitively that I was completely safe.

I stood up to greet him as we came face to face.

"Do I know you?" I asked.

"Do you not recognize me?" he asked in response, with a strange Scottish accent. It was clear that he was Scottish, but the way he spoke was different than what I was used to. His head was slightly tilted as if he was studying me.

"I'm sorry, my memory hasn't been what it should. Have we met before?"

"Aye, lass," he said, sounding sad. "We have."

"What is your name, sir?" I asked him.

He took a deep breath before saying, "Henry."

Henry? Why did that sound so familiar? I pondered the name for a few moments.

Then it registered.

"Henry, I think I have been having dreams about you," I said.

"Aye, me as well, lass," he replied.

He seemed so sad. It made my heart ache. The sensation came out of nowhere, and, as it struck me, everything around me shifted and shook, almost as if it was being disrupted in some way. Like a flame getting hit by a breeze without it being extinguished.

Henry looked around as if he had noticed it too.

"What was that?" I asked. "Why do you feel the way that you do? It's as if you are sad."

I was confused by this. Sadness was not something felt here. Only joy and happiness. Why was this man sad, and why could I feel it?

"I miss you," was all he said.

My response surprised me and left my lips before I could think to not ask, "And who is it that you miss?"

With one word my world literally came crashing down around me.

He stared at me intently and spoke in a whisper, "Annalyse."

I knew this name.

I suddenly remembered hearing it being screamed by this man standing in front of me, as I was being choked and had my head slammed against a wall. I remembered, it as a woman who looked like me spoke to me about my soul's purpose and my Mirror Soul.

Mirror Soul? This term replayed visions in my head of being struck by lighting and being split in two.

As these thoughts and memories invaded my mind like an infestation of some dark, biblical plague, I could feel the environment around me change. The sky turned dark with clouds, and lightning flashed, tearing through the sky as the pain all came pouring back and tore through my heart. I collapsed to the ground, to my knees, in agony.

"Annalyse!" the man named Henry shouted.

I looked up at him from the ground as lightning built inside my own body. I could feel rage growing inside me, looking for an escape.

"You," was all I said, as the disdain dripped from my lips.

Henry stared at me in shock.

Good, I thought.

I wanted him to suffer, to suffer like he had made me suffer. Like all men had made me suffer. The only man that had ever not made me suffer was Michael, and Henry couldn't just let me be at peace. He had to come drag me back through the pain and suffering caused by his kind.

I wanted nothing of it.

"Leave. Now." I said as my hands dug into the cool dirt beneath me feeling the energy of my environment building as I fed into it.

His attention quickly shifted to something behind me. I looked over my shoulder to see Michael walking across the field towards us.

He looked like a god. The wind whipped across his hair and clothes, while his bright blue eyes flashed as the lightning cut across the sky. I looked back up at Henry to see the look of shock and surprise on his face.

And was that fear?

Good.

Michael came up behind me and helped me up.

I felt better just having him close by, but the storm still raged around us.

"You should go," Michael spoke to Henry over my shoulder.

"I cannot. I cannot leave without her," Henry told Michael before directing his next statement to me. "Annalyse, please. You do not belong here. You need to come back. Come back to me."

I cringed back into Michael's arms and away from him. That was the only guidance Michael needed. He stepped in front of me and spoke again to Henry.

"You need to leave. Now. I will not ask again."

I could tell Henry was upset and confused, but I didn't care. I knew exactly who he was, and I didn't want to go back with him. I wanted to stay here with Michael. I was tired of the suffering. This was where I wanted to be.

"Annalyse," he tried again. "You belong with me. Please. Please come back."

"I belong with Michael," I said from behind Michael's large, strong body. "You just bring pain."

My words struck him like a blow that only temporarily slowed him down.

He then turned his attention back to Michael.

"You cannot have her. You had your time with her. This is not how it is supposed to be, I am supposed to give her what she needs, in our time, in our reality, in our dimension. She cannot heal here anymore. You have done all you can do. She cannot complete her journey without facing it."

Michael had no chance to respond, as the pain that had been building inside me fired off out of my mouth like a cannon blast.

"YOU ABANDONED ME!!!!" I screamed in rage, as my entire body shook with convulsions of hysterical fury. "If you had never left me in the first place, none of this would have ever happened! It's *all your fault! You* chose to leave me." My energy changed from range to sorrow as I fell to my knees again and began to cry. "You could have stayed. We could have been happy. But you left, and because of that Rose and I died." I looked up at him in accusation, "I had to kill her... because you weren't there. Did you know that? Do you not understand what the pain of your choices caused me? Caused us? How could I ever, possibly, forgive you? How could I possibly heal from what I did? How can I forgive myself?"

"But, Annalyse," Henry began, "yes, everything you are saying is true. I did all of those things. But so did Michael. We are the same. The difference is that he cannot make it right, but I can. We can. Together. We can make it all have been worth something. Not only did I come back this time, I have been fighting to get to you. I fought then to get to you, but I was too late, and I am so sorry. I may have left then, but I cannot leave now. I will not! Michael is an illusion. He cannot make things right – but I can, and I want to."

Tears began pouring down my face as I looked at Michael, while the truth of Henry's words washed over me. He was right. It was Michael who had abandoned me, yet it was Henry who was here, fighting to get me back.

Seeing my sorrow, Henry stepped forward in an effort to console me, but Michael had other plans. Henry hadn't made it forward but a few inches before Michael's fist collided with Henry's face. For a moment, I was taken aback, but then I felt a rush of pleasure that shocked and surprised me.

In this moment, I was able to see Michael step in to defend and protect me, where in the past he had been absent and unable to do so. My feelings were short-lived, as Henry quickly rebounded like he was someone who was used to sparing and fighting. Henry hit Michael with an uppercut that sent blood flying from his mouth as his head snapped back.

I watched these two men who both represented the same one, as they each fought for me. I found the situation to be ironic, as they took and threw punch after punch. Michael and Henry were one Being who in this moment were battling each other.

So, in reality, Henry was at war with himself, and Michael was also at war with himself. I guess it's true that we are our own biggest enemy. I watched and wondered how many other men were walking the earth at war with themselves without even being aware of it. Fighting themselves and the things that they had done that brought them shame and remorse, instead of healing. Hiding part of themselves in the shadows, afraid to let the light shine on their wounds, like the creatures I had seen not moments ago.

Watching this battle, I was able to see the genuine pain and anguish that men must walk around with and silently suffer under. Unable to face it or heal it because they fought so hard to keep it so tightly contained. The internal battle must be such a strong corrosive to their soul, proving to be some next level torment that they had no idea how to escape because they were never given to tools to do so. It was in this moment that I had compassion. I'd seen my own pain and it had clouded my ability to see theirs.

"STOP!" I screamed, as I witnessed Henry lock Michael's head under his arm. It looked as if he was poised to snap his neck.

My compassion had quickly been extinguished like a fire that had been doused with water. I hated Henry. I hated him for what he represented, I hated him for hurting Michael, but mostly I hated him for reminding me of the truth and making me have to face it. To face my destiny. To face more pain and suffering.

Henry lifted his head away from Michael's and looked at me straight in the eyes and said "I won't hurt you like this, Annalyse. Even to defeat my own demons, I would never intentionally cause you pain." He then let go of Michael and let him fall to the ground gasping for air.

I then ran over to Michael to tend to him and assess the damage. As I held Michael in my arms, I looked up at Henry in loathing. His reaction was not what I expected.

"I am sorry, Annalyse," he said. "Forcing you to choose me by default would not have been a victory for any of us. By destroying Michael, it would have destroyed us both, as well as you and me. Forgive me."

And with that, he disappeared.

It was like death by hanging, but on someone's words. I simply knelt there in disbelief, holding Michael, staring at the now empty space where Henry had been just a moment prior.

It was in that moment that I felt the empty space inside myself. Henry may have just left, but my destiny was still firmly in front of me and there was no running from it. I bent my head down and rested it on Michael's shoulder.

I felt his strong hand gently cradle the back of my head as I began to cry.

CHAPTER 18

Henry

I sat bolt upright, immediately, when I woke up and let out a guttural scream of rage and frustration before jumping out of bed to begin pacing back and forth.

Shannon and Morgan scurried back from me quickly, and I immediately felt badly that I had reacted in such an extreme way, scaring them. They were here trying to help me and Annalyse, and they did not deserve to be in the wake of my pain.

"What happened?!" Morgan asked. "Did you find her?"

I ran my hand through my hair in an effort to disperse some frustration energy before saying, "Aye."

I just stood there shaking my head as I replayed what had happened. It certainly did not go as I had hoped.

"Fuck," I muttered under my breath as I began pacing around again.

Morgan appeared directly in front of me and looking me straight in the eyes said, "Get yourself together Henry and tell us what the fuck happened."

I was momentarily stunned by her boldness and use of words. Morgan was a petite woman, but in that moment she was a force to be reckoned with. There was fire in her eyes, and she radiated power. I took several steps back as her energy pushed against me like a bulldozer.

"When I made it in, I found her swinging on a homemade swing attached to a large tree that stood alone in a field. It was a beautiful place, and everything was very peaceful. At first, she did not recognize me, just like the last time I had showed up as myself. To say it hurt like hell is an understatement. It was not until I said her name that something jogged her memory and it seemed as if everything came flooding back to her. She got very angry once she realized who I was. Then things got stormy, lighting zapped across the sky, and the wind picked up like we were in some blasted hurricane."

I paused for a moment and paced around a bit more not wanting to talk about what happened next – what I had almost done.

There was silence for a few moments, until Shannon broke it.

"Henry, tell us what happened," she pressed.

I looked at her and then at Morgan and then dropped my eyes, unable to look at either one of them.

"I almost killed him," I said in a whisper.

"Wait. What? Him?" Morgan said looking between Shannon and myself obviously confused, "Almost killed who?"

"Himself," Shannon answered for me.

I shot my eyes at her, "What?"

"Did you forget, Henry? Michael was and is you. Just a different physical expression in a different timeline. So, in essence, you almost killed yourself."

Her statement tip-toed around being a question, but just missed the mark, as she helped to clarify my original answer.

"Aye," I said sitting down in one of the chairs in front of the fireplace, hanging my head in disgust, "And right in front of Annalyse."

There was no response for some time. I imagined the women standing behind me, exchanging glances, condemning and judging me. I truly did not care. I deserved it.

Finally, Morgan broke the silence.

"Can someone please explain to me who Michael is?"

Before I could say anything, Shannon answered concisely.

"Henry and Annalyse know each other from a past life as Michael and Sara. They were reunited in this lifetime when Annalyse's soul entered into Henry's late wife, Vivien, when her soul departed in the car accident. Vivien's body was attacked the night before he came to Annalyse's room in the hospital, and she died. Annalyse's soul then returned to her own body, and, well, you know the rest."

More silence except the sound of footsteps making their way towards me. I stood up to turn around, just as my face was met by a hand colliding with it. I fell back into the chair feeling dazed.

In a normal situation, being slapped by someone a whole foot shorter than me would not have had much effect, but since Morgan took me by surprise and my footing was already unstable, her force took me down.

I placed my hand over the stinging skin just as Morgan stood in front of me and yelled, "YOU WERE WITH HER ALL THAT TIME AND KEPT HER TO YOURSELF, WHILE I WAS UP NIGHTS CRYING, WORRIED SICK ABOUT MY BEST FRIEND, NOT KNOWING WHAT WAS GOING ON!? AND YOU JUST LEFT HER BODY IN THE HOSPITAL, ALONE TO ROT?!"

I sat there paralyzed by her words and accusations.

I had already struggled under so much guilt about everything that had happened with Annalyse that I felt like I could mildly understand the cross that Jesus bore, as the weight of everyone was on it. I felt almost as weighed down. I could not argue with her or fight anymore. She did not ken everything that transpired between Annalyse and me and how much Annalyse suffered knowing Morgan was in pain mourning over her.

There was no point in explaining. It did not matter. Even if she did not ken my exact sins, I was still guilty of so many, that the condemnation was equally relevant, even if she did not ken for what charges I should be hung for.

My blank stare was not a satisfying answer to her, so she added, "You're a selfish bastard, and hope you're in as much pain as you've been carrying on like you're in. You deserve every second of it. Annalyse deserves better than you. No wonder she chose this *Michael* over you. It sounds like you evolved backwards from that lifetime instead of forward."

She then turned on her heal and left.

No wonder she chose Michael....

Those words bounced around in my head like an echo in a cavern, as I bent forward and rested my face in my hands.

I guess she was right.

Maybe I had failed. Maybe I had not done my own healing from having lost her before in that lifetime. It was clear to me that he was not the version of Michael who had been separated from her and had found her dead after tipping herself and our daughter off the edge of our bedroom balcony. Perhaps if he had been, he would have displayed the brokenness that I have been laboring under and acting from too.

It is so much easier to love someone when they are whole. It takes a whole other level of strength to be willing to help piece someone back together while getting cut on all their broken shards in the process. I was able to love Annalyse when she struggled to feel safe with intimacy with me. Would she still be able to love me while I struggled with intimacy with myself? How could she possibly love me now? I did not even love myself.

I failed her.

I failed us.

I failed everyone.

How many times had I been at fault for her being hurt?

Perhaps Morgan had been right. As much as I tried to get myself into a place of service, at the bottom of every action was my own selfish desire to have her back. The truth was, when I broke it all down, and looked at the most basic underlying reason I kept trying so hard, it was not because I wanted to be back in union – which, of course I did, and that desire has not changed – but it was because I wanted to fix what I had broken.

I wanted the chance to make things right. To fix us, to fix her. Shannon had been right all this time about my own wounding. I was being ruled by my

Warrior's Wound and seeking every path I could take to try to right my past wrongs so that I could believe that I deserved forgiveness and the type of love that Annalyse and I share. That has been the hardest lesson in all of this. Understanding that I do not honor Annalyse and her journey by trying to fix her. I honor her by simply standing in the gap for her, holding space for her, when she needs it, and loving her. I honor her in the same way I honor myself. I cannot give her what I do not have, and, if I cannot learn how to love myself unconditionally, then how could I love her without condition?

It was truly that simple, but here I had to go and do, do, do. I had to try to force and try to make things happen, and, as a result, I may have lost her forever and doomed humanity. Why is it so difficult to just sit with a woman in their pain without trying to fix it for them? I had been looking at Annalyse as if she were a problem that needed to be solved, instead of seeing her for what she truly is: the solution.

Shannon squatted down in front of me and gently placed her hand on my shoulder.

"Henry, tell me what happened."

I lifted my head and looked at her. I had not realized I had been crying until I saw the tears in my hands glistening against my skin like morning dew on a blade of grass.

"When she remembered me, she looked at me with the level of disgust I feel with myself for allowing what happened to her to happen. She hated me, Shannon. No wonder she does not want to come back. No wonder she does not want to be with me anymore." I sat there shaking my head as my statement hung in the air between us. "Shannon, even if she does come back, I think I have lost her forever."

"Henry, you don't know that. We don't know what will happen now, but I think you've learned what you need to do for her from this point forward, no matter what happens and no matter what she chooses, right?"

The way she looked at me and spoke to me made me feel like I was a child who had just learned a very valuable lesson in ethics by having had a seriously negative consequence and an equally massive tantrum as a result.

"Aye," I responded as fresh tears spilled over my waterlines and rolled down my cheeks. "At this point, I have nothing left to give her but the one and only thing she needs. My love."

Shannon stared at me, with tears in her own eyes, and simply nodded. She then leaned forward and gave me a hug. It was in that moment that I stopped fighting and felt the emotions I had tried so hard to run from bubble up inside me, craving their escape. I had been a fool thinking I could keep myself so busy and occupied with fixing everything that I could escape the pain.

It tore through me like a hot whip made purely out of flame. It sliced my heart, while also cauterizing the wound at the same time. It was almost as if the pain was my salvation, and the only way to heal was to accept it, feel it, and move through it.

So that is exactly what I did.

I was grateful for Shannon and all that she had done for me though this. I was mostly grateful for her to lean on in this moment.

After a few minutes, Shannon released me, stood up, and sat down in the other chair. She said nothing, and simply let me sit with my pain for a little while. I am not sure how much time passed, as I marinated in my misery, before I felt a strange sensation on my leg.

My phone had buzzed in my pocket, so I pulled it out to see that I had received a text from a number that I had not stored.

"Who is it?" Shannon asked.

"I do not ken," I said as I tapped on the message.

I opened the text message and quickly read it. Once I was done reading it, I let my hand drop down to my side and stared off into space, trying to make sense of what I had just read.

"Was it Morgan?" Shannon asked.

"No," I said, as I turned my head to look at her. "It was Annie."

CHAPTER 19

"Don't weep, my darling," Michael said as he stroked the back of my head. "Everything is fine now. Everything will be ok. Do not fuss. I'm here."

He kept trying to comfort me, as he gently rocked me back and forth in the grass.

The thing was, he didn't understand what was tearing my heart out. Now that Henry was gone the sky had cleared. The sun had completely set now, yet I could still see remnants of its light reflecting on the horizon. The combination of the pink and purple sky and the newly-awakened stars was the perfect example of my heart. Though the stars were there, they could never truly shine to their fullest potential until the sky fully released the sun.

I realized now that this was the choice Theia was referring to. All this time, I was not fully able to move forward, to be completely in union with Henry and our mission because I was still holding on to Michael.

Though Michael and Henry were the same soul expression, just physical manifestations in different lifetimes, the ache I had experienced from the loss of Michael was something that had not fully been healed by finding Henry in my current life. There was a part of me that blamed Henry for this, but, in truth, it wasn't his fault.

It was the wounding of that loss that I was not willing to release. It had been part of my identity for so long that I didn't know how to release it. Even as I was with Henry, there was an echo of disconnection. I now understood that this disconnection was caused by me. So long as there was a part of me that still saw myself as a victim of the universe who had lost this great love, I could never truly step into my full power as a whole woman.

I had to let Michael go.

I had to finally release him so that the part of Henry that was Michael could reassimilate into the whole and so that I could fully merge into Henry's and my union. What I hadn't realized was that, by holding onto Michael, I was keeping both Henry and myself fractured. Henry had been right. By destroying

Michael, he would have destroyed us both because Michael was a part of both of us. By holding onto him I was keeping Henry a broken man.

Because I kept trying to make Henry pay for what he did in the past and I held onto a victim energy from it, I was also energetically anchoring him to that space and time as well. How could we ever grow and find peace in our future, if I was holding us locked in a painful past?

I pulled back from Michael's embrace and looked him deeply in the eyes. We were now purely illuminated by the full moon and the stars. I could see the stars reflected in his eyes, and it made me long for home. Not physical home, but the one where my soul was completely returned to the universe and one with it.

"That's the thing, Michael. You aren't here. Henry was right. You're just an illusion. An echo of an energy that once was but is no longer in existence. You are a mental projection shining through the cracks of a broken heart. An empty promise, as fulfilling as sand in a canteen of water in the middle of the dessert. Yet, I still hold onto the canteen because I think that somehow it will finally slake my thirst.

I've been wanting from you what you cannot give me because it was never yours to give. I put the very essence of my wholeness into the hands of the wisp of a memory whose only true existence was that which occurred in my own head."

I touched the side of Michael's face, in the hopes of etching every single detail of him into my brain. He watched my face intently as I soaked him in.

"The thing I have come to realize is that the longer I go without seeing your true essence as Henry, my feelings for *you* become more like the edge of an echo that no longer brings satisfaction and only the pain of loss and the reminder of what was... what could have been, but isn't.

Even when I was with Henry, it was like the ghost of my lover was still there, because *you* were not. You were here. Still existing in my broken heart and the identity I had grown so attached to that was filled with the pain of our separation. I have held on to the loss of you for so long that I have not been able to move on from it. Even now, the love that I have for you is so real to me, but I know that it is but a resonance of what once was.

I cannot stay here with you anymore. I must move forward. I cannot reach my highest potential while still trying to hold onto such deeply-rooted pain. I've held onto that pain and loss for so long, fearing that if I let you go you will fade away, when, in truth, by releasing you, I can finally find you again."

Somehow, I instinctively knew what I needed to do, so I stood up and offered him a hand to help him up.

Holding his hand, we began walking.

"So now you ken," Michael said.

What?

I came to an abrupt stop and turned to look at him.

"You knew?" I asked him with confusion and mild accusation.

"Aye, my darling. I've chased you through lifetimes. Once I'd heard, as Michael, that you had left the physical realm, I immediately chased after you in the spirit realm, but when I got there you had already reincarnated. I've stayed an incomplete man to be here for you in this space because I kenned you would need me to be here for you at this point of our journey. I would stay here with you forever, condemned to a half-life on the other side, if that's what you needed from me."

"Is that why I could recognize you in Henry, but I still couldn't *feel* you? Because this version of yourself has been stuck? Trapped? So that I could find you here? So you would be here for me when I needed to heal?"

"Aye, Henry and I are but two expressions of the same soul, experiencing life in two different dimensions. Once you release me, there is no longer a need for this version of myself to remain here and I can assimilate back into my whole self. You will feel me in Henry then because I will no longer exist here. Only in him."

I looked off across the horizon while I contemplated his words.

The endless view, mirroring the endless love that this man had for me. Imagine loving someone so much that you would allow part of your own soul identity and essence to remain in a past life experience so that it would be there for another when they needed it as a mental and emotional safe haven. I was stunned. Michael loved me that much.

Henry loved me that much.

And it was time.

Because I loved him that much too.

"What is it, my beloved?" he asked.

I turned to look at him and said, "I'm so sorry Michael. I have been so selfish holding on to you for so long, not allowing you to find your rest or peace. I understand where the feeling of separation from you comes from as I now see that I have been holding you trapped here in this time and space, instead of allowing you to move on and return to the whole."

As I spoke, I could see multiple reactions spread across his face. A combination of sadness and relief told me that he knew I was speaking the truth.

"My darling, I would split my soul into a thousand pieces and hide each piece away in different realms, times, and realities, if that is what you needed from me. If that was what was needed to find my way back to you. If that was what you needed to find your way back to yourself. Back to us. I would do whatever it takes."

"I know," I replied. "But, see Michael, the problem with splitting your soul is that it is also mine, and I feel the separation too. I thought the only way to be with you was to be here with you, but that's not true. Even with Henry, I felt separated from you because I forced you to stay separate from him so that I could hold onto the wounded identity that I had known all my current life. By my not being willing to release the identity of victimhood around our loss and separation, I continued to create the paradigm in which we were indeed separate, and, by keeping you separate, I have been keeping Henry from being whole too. I'm so sorry."

Michael stroked my cheek and said, "There is nothing to apologize for. You're healing. Never apologize for doing that work."

I stepped forward towards him and placed my hands on his chest and closed my eyes for a moment, while I felt his heartbeat against my palms.

"Michael," I said, as I opened my eyes to peer deep into his. "I have loved you every day of my life. I have missed you and longed for you from the moment my heart began to beat in the new physical body I was born into. Though I never understood the connection, I felt it. Even as a child, I remembered you. I would sit in front of my nightlight and silently cry for you, longing for you to come find me and take me home. I always knew that you were out there, but what I had never pieced together was the fact that you were also inside me. It was my own separation with the truth of who and what I am that has kept me in this state of pain and separation for so long. I now call back to me all the pieces of myself that I have given to you and return to you all that I have taken from you."

Once I spoke the final words, a bright light began to blossom from both of our chests. It was so bright that I had to close my eyes tightly. Once I could tell that the light had dimmed and faded, I opened my eyes, began taking steps backwards, and said, "Thank you Michael for your role and part in my journey, and I now release you. Go. Rest. Find your peace. I love you."

As I slowly backed away from him, I could see a serene smile spread across his face, just as my foot encountered the edge of the cliff that I had been backing up to. The last thing I saw, as I fell back over the edge of the world that I had created, was the peaceful face of Michael as he faded away into golden-white stardust.

As I fell, I could feel heat buildup in my body. I imagined I was a cosmic entity entering the earth's atmosphere at high velocity and being caught on fire as I crossed through. As the heat built, it began to scare me, as it brought back cellular and soul memories of my soul crossing though fire to leave my body in the past. Now it seemed as if it needed to cross through fire to reenter it.

I clenched my teeth tight and squeezed my eyes shut in an attempt to prepare my body for the blistering pain that I awaited to come. But it never did. It was then that I realized that, as I passed through the fire it wouldn't consume me. I would consume it. My body was becoming it, and when I passed all the way through it, I would be ablaze with power and the magic of transfiguration.

They may have burned me once, but I am a Phoenix. Through their flames, I found my transformation power, and now it was time to share it with the world. Now that the fire was a part of me and no longer something to be feared, every step I would take would light the way for others. I would become a walking beacon for hope, no longer fearing what would be attracted to my light, knowing that it would be so bright and high-vibrational that no bugs would want to come anywhere near it.

Once I finally just surrendered, I realized that it wasn't the transformation that causes pain; it's the trying to stay the same that does. It's the fighting against the natural evolution of our soul that generates the disconnect and causes us to suffer. Sometimes we can't transform into a healed state because we are trying so hard to hold onto the belief that we aren't hurt and don't need to heal. It's in the surrender that the true transformation can begin.

I opened my eyes to see warm, golden-orange light all around me. I could feel the flames swirling inside me and imagined that if I had a mirror, I would see them dancing in my eyes. I would also see something I had never truly allowed myself to see. I would see myself. I would see who I truly was. It was as if I could finally just be me. The exhilaration I felt at this realization only amplified the energy that surrounded me.

I was in a cocoon of fire and I finally surrendered to my metamorphosis. No more fighting. I finally felt what I had so desperately craved to feel my entire life. Love. A deep, rooted love that came from none other than myself. There it was: the key to unlock the rest of my journey. It's as if allowing my love to be felt for myself and given to myself freely was truly what I had been seeking all this time. It wasn't Michael or Henry, it was me.

We all begin our journey in different places, but, in this moment, I realized that the first step in the right direction was to love one's self. Once that happened, the rest would take care of itself, and I was ready for it. I had chosen this path, and it was time to become what I was destined to be.

I gasped as I woke up to the sight of three familiar faces staring back at me.

"Welcome back," one of them said, as they all smiled proudly at me.

Well, sort of smiled. I at least assumed that the white lion faces were smiling at me. Either that, or they thought I was a tasty morsel that was ready to be devoured.

Theia and the Royal Lions, Regulus and Sirius, were looking down on me with admiration and anticipation.

I personally was in shock.

How was I still here?

"What happened?" I asked, as I started making my way into an upright position, while one of the white lions offered me a thick paw to use as leverage.

Sitting on the table with my legs hanging over the edge, I looked at each of them until Theia spoke.

"You tell us."

This shit again? Was she fucking joking? Here I thought I was done with all of this and I was on my way back to Henry, only to find out that I had simply been taking a nap? For the love of god.

"Theia, I'm not really in the mood for more of your riddles and subtle implications that I know more than I actually do."

To my surprise, she smiled at me. It was as if she enjoyed my cheekiness and found it entertaining. Almost as an adult finds the ornery musings of a child humorous. Her response did nothing to temper the flames that I could feel still burning inside me.

"Here, let me help you," she offered, as she held out her hand for me to take hold of.

I cut my eyes in suspicion at her offer to assist me. As much as she had tried to let on that she was there for me as a guide, I felt about as supported by her as I would be going braless.

Maintaining eye contact with her, I extended my hand and allowed her to take it and lead me over to the same archway where I had seen the thick black substance and witnessed the Vision of Origination. Only this time the surface was that of a mirror. I stared at myself in shock. There were flames dancing all around me, licking and flicking my skin. My hair was bright orange and vibrant and it danced around behind me as if wind were floating through it.

No wonder I felt as though flames were building and burning inside me. They actually were.

"What is this?" I asked, as I turned my head to look at her.

It was interesting seeing us standing side by side in this mirror now. When I had first met her, I thought she was the most miraculous and remarkable thing. A version of myself that I felt I could never possibly attain. But now, here I was standing side by side with her, and she was the one looking rather ordinary, while I looked like some mythical Goddess of Fire.

She smirked as she watched me, almost as if she could hear my thoughts. Knowing she was, in fact, me, she probably could.

"This," Theia responded as she stared at my reflection next to hers, "is you."

I glared at her own reflection in response to her, yet again, cryptic and unexplanatory "explanation."

Laughing she replied, "Well, alright. This is the real you. I presume you have heard of the mythical being called a Phoenix?" Chuckling again, she added, "Of course you have, and, of course, I know you have."

God, was I this annoying, really? Ugh.

"Well," she continued, "the Phoenix was a fable that was created based off you. Off *us*."

I turned my head in surprise to look directly at her.

"What?"

"Yes," she responded, while still looking at the reflected version of me. "Do you remember the spell you recited over Ky before he transitioned?"

"Yes."

For some reason I felt compelled to speak it again. Only this time, I spoke it to my reflection in the mirror.

"I had a dream about you and me. We were a large, beautiful tree. A tree of life. The Tree of Life. We were massive, strong, and so intertwined in each other's energies that you could not tell one from the other. We were once the same and it was just us.

Do you remember?

Then the lightning struck, and we were torn apart. Both halves of the tree falling away from each other, turning black and unyielding of the fruit we were designed to make. You going left and me going right. We crashed onto the broken earth like a canon blast. Or was that the sound of my heart breaking? Our heart breaking.

Did you hear it too?

We searched for one another. Looking. Seeking. Growing our branches as they stretched across the barren wasteland. At last, we found each other, but we didn't recognize the other. Our branches simply grew and raged against one another. We were fighting each other.

Could you feel it?

The pain was unbearable. You tried to swallow me up and overtake me. You tried to destroy me. This destroyed us both, for your war on me was a war on you, as we were both the same.

Are both the same.

Then, the fire came. It shot from the earth at the space where we were torn apart. It healed us. It raged, a tower-like inferno that rained down its purification and cleansing. The earth began to wake up. Turning green and blue with life. Breathing remembrance into our branches.

Don't I know you?

Finally, from this Flame was born a new tree. A small tree, but a strong tree, and we became its roots. Its heritage. Its lineage. Its memories. We became the new tree. Finally, we found each other again. We are now returned to our true nature.

Why can't you remember?

Wake up, beloved. There is much work to do. The roots are whispering to me. Hear, listen, remember. I'm tired of fighting. I surrender my will to try to make you be anything other than what you were meant to be. I don't know what more to do.

So, I'm just going to love you."

After I finished speaking the words, I watched as the surface of the mirror shifted. It was almost as if it became like mercury, a fluid silver substance, before solidifying itself again. Only once it was back to a solid state, I was no longer looking into my own reflection, but that of Henry's.

Henry….

Confused for a moment, I looked down at my own hands and body thinking I must have transformed into him, but I had not. I was still the flaming goddess I had gazed upon a few moments ago. Taking my hand that I was just examining, I placed it on the surface of the mirror where it would have been on Henry's heart.

"Theia, help me understand," I said, as I turned my head to look over my shoulder at her. Only she wasn't there. Standing in her place was Henry. Or at least Henry's higher self, Ky.

Confused, I looked back at the mirror to see myself reflected once more.

I placed both of my hands on the surface this time and gazed deeply into myself.

"Tell me what I need to know."

To my surprise, it was Henry's higher self who responded from behind me.

"After the lightning struck and split us apart into physical expressions of male and female energy, there was pain. We both remember this on a deep cellular level."

I nodded at the truth of his statement but remained quiet to encourage him to continue.

"When the fire came, many thought it was the end of everything. The earth exploded with fire, magma, and ash. The truth was, this was not the end, but a beginning. A birthing from the core of Gaia. It was her very essence that we had fed, nurtured, and grew within the root system that belonged to the very tree that was attacking itself. It was within this own tree's deepest, darkest parts where its own healing resided.

The Earth was incubating the magic and power of *the* Divine Feminine, within her womb, and gave birth to Her at the very site where we had become broken apart – the site now referred to as Devil's Tower. A fitting term to go with the constant demonizing by the patriarchal energy that worked for so long to oppress this magic and all who wielded it.

When the explosion happened, there arose a fiery being that immerged from the earth. It rose in the flames and spread its arms wide open. For those that did not understand what was truly happening, the creature looked like a large, flaming bird flying out of the earth. It was only after her appearance that things began to improve. This began the age where women were revered and seen as wise and magical. They were honored as mystics and goddesses in human form. For thousands of years, women ruled the planet. There was peace, prosperity, health and wellbeing, and harmony with the planet. It was years before the masculine became jealous and fearful of their powers to create and to make and wield magic."

"And then they condemned us for it," Theia spoke from within the mirror that was reflecting my true self, diverting my attention away from Henry's higher self. "They then suppressed us and stole our magic. For thousands of years they have taken our sacred symbols and perverted them to use them to work dark magic against us. To work evil deeds and fool those who are unaware of the true meaning behind the symbols convincing them that those who still wield them for their proper use are witches to be feared, isolated, and even eliminated as a threat to society. It's those that speak against the 'norm' for the abomination that it is and who see through the fog and the veil and identify the agenda and farce for its lies; it is them they seek to destroy. People think that the witch hunts have ended, but they are wrong. They are still happening today to the real magic workers. To anyone fighting to break the paradigm that has held humanity prisoner for thousands of years."

I knew this to be true. I saw it for myself when friends would call out corrupt agendas that were set up and staged to gain control of the people and turn them against those who could see through the mind control and manipulation. People in power pitting brother and sister against each other and sprinkling fear and chaos into their midst. The thing was, this was so much bigger than me. How could I stop this or make any difference at all?

"What am I to do?" I asked as I leaned into my own reflection.

"It is time for a new beginning. The Divine Feminine must rise again."

I turned around, as it was Henry's higher self who answered my question, and looked at him terrified.

"What are you saying?"

He stepped forward and gently took my hand.

"Annalyse, it's time."

"Time for what?" I asked, feeling my heart rate begin to increase in my chest. It was less like a pounding and more like a fluttering. I took deep breaths to try to calm myself. I had felt my heart do this off and on my whole life. More so when I was a child, but now and then as an adult. It was like it stopped beating for a moment or two and just spasmed as electricity charged through it. Deep, calm breathing tended to help.

"It's time to stop hiding. It's time to step into who you truly are."

"I'm not ready. I don't even know how or what that means."

Henry's higher self stepped closer to me and took both of my hands in his and held them between our hearts. Then looking deeply into my eyes he said, "It's ok. *I'm* ready and I am here to help you."

"How?"

"You came here to remind me who I am. Now it's my turn to remind you. I will help you remember. I will help complete the task we both came here to see through. But first, my love" he paused for a moment to kiss me in the center of my forehead, causing me to close my eyes. Then leaning his forehead against my own, he whispered, "it's time to wake up."

CHAPTER 20
Henry

I found it ironic how often I found myself running down the halls of this god forsaken hospital. I truly had begun to hate this place. The sights, the smells, they were all associated with heartache and pain. It felt easier to run this time, now that my body was rested and my mind had been able to have some time to reboot.

The text I had received from Annie had been like getting hit with a taser right in the heart. Apparently when she had been checking in on Annalyse's stats, Annalyse's heart rate began to climb alarmingly fast for no obvious reason. It was as if she had begun her own sprint and her heart had been pounding as hard as mine was now. Annie had run to get the doctor and by the time they had returned everything seemed to be back to normal.

Well, normal for what had been going on with her.

I kenned something had happened though. Something changed. Our encounter in her dreamscape had been very intense, and my heart squeezed at the idea that I may have caused her so much turmoil that it affected her physical body in such a way.

After reaching her door, I found Annie looking in on her.

"Mr. McLauhlan!" she said as she turned around in surprise. "I didn't expect to see you here."

Oh? I paused for a second. I guess that made sense. Annie only kenned me as someone who was concerned about the victim of an accident that was technically my fault. Clearly by this point she had realized there was more between us than that, but, remaining professional, never inquired.

"That was sweet of you to come to check in on her," Annie said.

"Aye. It felt like the right thing to do," I replied, unsure of what exactly to say.

She simply nodded and gave me a gentle smile.

"Have there been any other changes or any new behaviors?" I asked standing there awkwardly.

"No sir. Beside that one anomaly, everything else seems to have settled back down to what it had been."

Her answer was what I expected but not what I wanted to hear.

"Thank you, do you mind if I stay for a little while?" I asked, motioning towards the chair.

"I think that should be fine," Annie answered. "Let me know if anything changes."

"Aye. Of course. Absolutely."

I sat down in the chair next to Annalyse and then turned to watch Annie leave the room. Once I was sure we were alone and I was able to speak openly, I place my hand on hers and gently enveloped hers in mine.

Her skin felt surprisingly warm. It concerned me for a moment, so I gently felt her cheeks and forehead, trying to get a read on her temperature. She felt like she was burning up.

I quickly stood up and walked out to the nurse's station to find Annie. My heart sank when she was not there. As I turned to head back to Annalyse's room, I almost walked right into Annie.

"Oh, my goodness!" she said as she dropped a file she had been holding. I bent down to pick it up.

Fortunately, it appeared as if all the materials inside where all still in their rightful home and had not strewn themselves all over the floor.

"I'm so sorry!" she said. "I was coming up behind you to ask if everything was ok. I didn't realize you would turn so quickly. Thank you," she added as she accepted the return of her file.

"It's ok Annie, I was actually coming to find you because I felt Annalyse's skin, and she felt very warm to the touch. Almost as if her skin were on fire. I'm worried she may have a high fever."

"Really?" she asked surprised. "I hadn't noticed anything in particular when I just checked in on her."

We started heading back to Annalyse's room, and once we arrived, Annie placed a temperature reader in Annalyse's ear to read her temperature. When it beeped, she looked at me and said, "Ninety-eight point two," with a bewildered shrug. "I wouldn't call the point two, instead of it reading point one, a fever. Everyone has a normal temperature, and she's within that range."

"That's so strange," I told her, as I gently placed my hand on Annalyse's cheek. "See," I said, as I motioned for Annie to feel Annalyse's cheek. "Doesn't she feel hot?"

Annie's expression grew bewildered as she felt Annalyse's cheeks.

"Yes, yes she does."

"What do you think it means?" I asked trying to stay calm.

"I'm honestly not sure. As she doesn't seem to have a fever, I don't think it's anything to worry about. Let me know if anything changes, ok?" She gently rested her hand on my shoulder for a second and gave me a look that showed that she kenned why I was really there and that she had compassion for me.

I nodded and said, "Of course. Oh, and thank you."

She smiled again and then left the room.

"Oh, my neach-gaoil, what is going on with you?" I asked as I sat back down in the chair next to Annalyse's bed.

I touched her warm hand again and lifted it to my cheek to place her palm against my skin then looked at her beautiful face. Her skin was so lovely. Like milk with a little bit of sunshine mixed in. I had not noticed that before. It was almost as if she glowed. Her red hair looked like flames curling around her lovely face. I longed to look into her eyes. To truly see her. I just hoped that in that moment she could truly see me too.

"My beloved, where to begin with an apology to you?" I began. "My weakness when you needed my strength is a shame I struggle with forgiving myself. But I know I must, for how could I expect you to give me something that I cannot give myself? Your strength amazes me. You are like a goddess who has come to this world to bring balance and suffered tremendously under its imbalances. But I know you are strong enough to rise. It is your time now, my Anam Faileas."

I took a deep breath and then brought her hand to my lips and kissed it. I had not realized I had started crying until I saw the tiny droplet on the back of her hand as I lowered it back down.

"Oh Annalyse," I continued. "I am so sorry. I am sorry that I could not be the man that you needed me to be. I am sorry that I was too weak to walk through the fires with you and have instead stood by the sideline panicking, trying to figure out a way to get you out. I am sorry that I could not honor your journey and that, instead of simply loving you through it and standing by your side, I constantly looked for ways to fix things as a means of escaping them. I am sorry that I saw your healing as a problem that needed to be fixed instead of simply allowing it and supporting you.

Through your journey, I have discovered so much of my own. You have shown me the strength that lies in letting go. The power that comes from surrender. Your bravery and courage have inspired me, and I know it will inspire millions. I am honored to get to witness the magic that you will bring to this world when you return to it, for you belong to them, not to me. I have been so selfish in wanting you to be back for me to have you, instead of allowing you to do the work that you need to do in order for you to fulfill your soul's purpose to all."

I lifted her hand again and held it in both hands and said, "I'm here now. Whenever you are ready, wake up beloved. I am tired of fighting. I surrender my will to try to make you be anything other than what you were meant to be. I do not know what more to do. So, I'm just going to love you."

I sat there with her for hours watching her chest rise and fall. I was concerned. To an outsider, nothing would have seemed out of the ordinary, but I could feel in her energy that something has happening. I kept having the thoughts creep into my mind that she and Michael were being intimate again, and I tried to cast them out as quickly as they came.

I thought of it as when I need to close apps in my phone, just swipe up and get rid of it. I just could not seem to cancel the thoughts fast enough. The energy felt so much like the same transformative energy we shared when I had tapped into

Michael's energy a few days ago. It was intense and I could feel how connected she was to everything and to me. I wondered too if this is why her body felt so warm, as if she were exerting herself in some way.

Stop, Henry. Swipe up.

A noise distracted me from my self-inflicted torment and I turned to see Morgan standing in the gap she created when she opened the door. My body went rigid as she glared at me.

I stood up to face her and said, "I will leave so you can spend some time with her without having to suffer my company."

My comment was only met with a sharp and chilling glare. It took much restraint from me to not shiver in response.

Morgan may be mad at me, but I was still ever grateful for her and the fact that Annalyse had a friend who cared for her so passionately to the level that she could put even a mother lioness to shame with her loyalty and ferocity.

I bent down to give Annalyse a kiss on her forehead and then turned to take my leave.

As suspected, Morgan's desire for my absence was confirmed when she made it clear that she was more than happy to hold the door open for me, and possibly even more pleased to close it swiftly behind me.

Once the door snapped shut behind me, I could immediately feel a swell of anxiety and longing consume me. It was pure agony being parted from Annalyse, and it took every fiber of strength I had in me to slowly make my way through the labyrinth that was the hospital.

By the time I reached the doors and stepped outside, I found it harder and harder to breath. Each breath ripping across the gaping hole in my chest that was there due to Annalyse's absence, causing additional pain.

It was not until I was fully submerged in the fresh oxygen that surrounded me that I began to feel slight relief. I had not realized how much I had been feeling like I was drowning until the air became easier to breathe. I looked up at the sky and took a deep, clearing breath, allowing myself to be fully present in that moment and I was so grateful to feel the fresh air on my face as I reached the parking lot. Oddly, for the first time in my life, the breath felt fully satisfying.

The drive home was filled with heartache, as it was very difficult leaving Annalyse. But I kenned Morgan wanted time with her, and though she thought I was a monster, I was not, and I would not deny her that time together. It was obvious she loved Annalyse dearly, and I was grateful to have someone to trade shifts with.

When I got home, I found Shannon running down the driveway to meet me. I rolled down my window and stopped the car as soon as we reached each other.

"Shannon! What is it!?" I asked frantically.

"Henry! I have been trying to reach your but your phone just kept going straight to voicemail."

I looked at my phone and realized I had forgotten to turn it back on after leaving the hospital.

Shit.

I looked at Shannon seriously, "What happened? What's wrong?"

She worked to catch her breath and pulled out her phone. "A message came through on the Smart Home unit, I'm assuming because you didn't receive it on your phone. I saw it and took a picture of it."

Holding up her phone, I could see a picture of Aine's, screen and as my brain interpreted what I saw, I felt like someone had cracked an egg on my head, and I could feel the wet yolk running down my body.

On the screen was another text message from Annie that read: "Mr. McLauhlan, she's awake."

I looked at Shannon and said, "Get in."

CHAPTER 21

I woke up, feeling like I had just been slammed back into my body, to the same beeping sound that was now becoming so familiar to me.

A heart rate monitor.

I took a moment to try to remember what had happened that landed me here. I remembered a lot of white, but nothing more until the memories flashed through my mind of the two men on the street, like a vivid nightmare, but instead of one you wake up from, I fell asleep to.

I then remembered saving a drowning man from a pool in a crystal cavern, talking to a woman who looked like me who referred to herself as Theia, my Higher Self, witnessing myself as an other worldly being, being split in two and being with Michael.

These images flashed in my head like pictures that had been let lose to fly in the wind.

Michael.

I jerked my eyes open and looked around the room for him. My eyes stopped on a familiar face, but it wasn't Michael.

"Oh my god! Annalyse! NURSE!," she yelled looking over her shoulder. "NURSE!"

Morgan paused for a moment as she watched me dart my eyes around as I began to panic from the feeling of the feeding tube in my throat.

"Hang on, Annalyse. Hang on. Stay calm. They are coming."

From the corner of my eye, I could see two nurses running into the room followed by a doctor. They neared my bed and began fiddling with tubes.

Suddenly things became foggy, and I felt as if I was falling back off to sleep. In what felt like only a few heart beats, I opened my eyes again feeling very relaxed and dazed, but not enough to not notice the fact that the tube had been removed from my throat.

Looking around, I found the anchor I was seeking in the tempest I was adrift in.

"Morgan?" I barely croaked in a whisper. "Morgan what happened? Where am I? Where's Michael?"

Morgan looked at me with concern as if she was unsure how to answer my question.

"Honey," she said holding my hand, "you were in a severe car accident and have been in a coma for just about two months." She paused for a moment to let the information sink in before asking in a worried tone, "Who is it that you're wanting?"

Who indeed? I found the wording of her question to be strange, but I moved past that quickly.

I merely stared at her as the realization hit me. It was MY voice I was speaking in. It was MY hand that she was holding.

I let my head fall back against the pillow as the heartache washed over me.

It wasn't real. None of it was real.

Michael was gone.

It had all just been another dream, though this time the dream was brought on by a massive head injury.

I hadn't noticed the tears running down my cheeks until her hand touched one of them gently to wipe it away.

"Oh, honey I'm so sorry. The good news is the doctors say you should make a full recovery. Your body has pretty much fully healed, and I've been taking good care of you. I knew you wouldn't want to look a hot mess when you woke up," she said with a tender smile. "We were all just so worried that you were still in the coma, as the doctors couldn't find any medical reason why you still would be. Thank God you woke up!"

"Yeah…" I croaked as my thoughts drifted off into oblivion.

We sat in silence for what felt like hours but may have only been minutes, as I allowed myself to immerse in what I felt were memories of the time Michael and I had together in this alternate reality that I had created.

Morgan said nothing, she simply sat next to me, with my hand in hers, holding space for me. It was as if she was some etheric tether that was holding me to earth because, without her, I felt so detached from my humanity that my soul may well have just floated away to find the feeling of home it so longed for, and temporarily had felt.

At some point, I started crying again, so Morgan leaned over to gently hug me.

I took advantage of her emotional response and allowed it to disguise my own. I had truly believed I had not only gotten confirmation of the existence of my true beloved, but that we were finally reunited, and even just thinking about him so deeply stirred up butterflies in my stomach. I could feel them longing to connect with him, but how? How could I possibly connect with this man who I only knew in my dreams?

The pain of the reality was too much. It was as if Michael and I had been separated all over again. Like he had died all over again.

I kept my eyes closed as the tears poured down my face, hiding my sorrow in my friend's embrace, unable to communicate to her what I was really experiencing and the loss I was feeling.

I had thought it was all real.

I had thought that Michael was real, and the release of him was real, and that there would be some type of purpose in the pain. That I would finally be reunited with my beloved soul mate. My Mirror Soul. But alas, it was all still just an illusion.

Michael, in this moment, seemed as real as the reflection in a mirror. Something I could see but never quite grasp.

A projection of myself onto a blank canvas.

Nothing more.

After a few minutes of being held, as I tried to emotionally process the loss of Michael, there was a sudden disturbance outside my room that pulled my attention away from my sorrow. It sounded like footsteps pounding on the hard, hospital floor as if someone were running.

Suddenly a man burst into the room and then froze at the sight of me.

I couldn't believe my eyes.

I was looking at a tall, handsome man with blue eyes and strawberry blonde hair.

He looked at me as tears built in the waterline of his eyes. His attention then slipped over to Morgan. I followed his gaze. Morgan looked between the two of us with concern and then stared at him with contempt.

Strange.

Morgan looked highly defensive and did not seem as if she wanted him here.

"It's okay," I said. "Can you please give us a moment?"

She nodded then stood up to walk out, looking at me with concern.

I nodded in reassurance. I loved her so much, but I couldn't wait to get her out of the room.

As she walked past him, she stared at him scathingly, which I found to be very odd. He didn't seem to notice as his attention was fully back on me.

His eyes burned as he looked at me. To see the fire magnified by the water gathering in his eyes made the butterflies in my solar plexus dance and I felt a cord just below my belly button tighten as if I'd just realized it's connection to him.

He took a guarded step forward and spoke fiercely, but in barely a whisper.

"Annalyse? Is it truly you?"

His voice trembled as he spoke the words.

I stared at him wide-eyed as my own tears blossomed to meet his in response to his deep emotion. It was as if I could feel what he felt.

I hadn't realized I had been holding my breath until the words gushed out of me on the winds of relief.

"Yes," I responded. "It is. But who are you?"

End of Book Two

Made in the USA
Coppell, TX
25 July 2021

59361870R10219